Jas felt re

She knew Harry ... the window ledge waiting to meet him. The deception made her feel like crawling under the mattress and never coming out.

On top of that, she felt guilty. The guy was having genuine feelings about her and she was spying on him. Despite the fact she must seem like a nut to him, he liked her.

What's more, she felt the same way about him. And here she was, finally in the position of meeting a guy she really liked, and what did she do about it? Lie to him. Spy on him. And then report back to the man who was out to ruin him. Talk about guilt!

And underneath the humiliation and the guilt there was the bottom layer of exhilaration that had been there ever since she kissed him. God, it had been ages since she felt like that about a man....

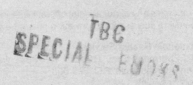

ABOUT THE AUTHOR

Beverly Sommers still likes living alone, red furniture and neon palm trees, and combines all of the above on her houseboat in Miami. Her favorite setting for books, though, is New York City. She feels that if you're not a native New Yorker, being set down in the city is like a great adventure.

Books by Beverly Sommers

HARLEQUIN AMERICAN ROMANCE

11–CITY LIFE, CITY LOVE
26–UNSCHEDULED LOVE
62–VERDICT OF LOVE
69–THE LAST KEY
85–MIX AND MATCH
125–CHANGING PLACES
137–CONVICTIONS
152–SNOWBIRD
165–LE CLUB
179–SILENT NIGHT
191–PHOEBE'S DEPUTY

HARLEQUIN INTRIGUE

3–MISTAKEN IDENTITY

Don't miss any of our special offers. Write to us at the following address for information on our newest releases.

Harlequin Reader Service
901 Fuhrmann Blvd., P.O. Box 1397, Buffalo, NY 14240
Canadian address: P.O. Box 603,
Fort Erie, Ont. L2A 5X3

Of Cats and Kings
Beverly Sommers

Harlequin Books

TORONTO • NEW YORK • LONDON
AMSTERDAM • PARIS • SYDNEY • HAMBURG
STOCKHOLM • ATHENS • TOKYO • MILAN

To Krissie,
who swore Deby would like this,
and to Deby, who did

Published September 1987

First printing July 1987

ISBN 0-373-16216-2

Chapter One

It was far and away the most popular comic strip in New York. It depicted Grogan, a streetwise cat. In a time when cats in general were popular, Grogan, who championed Everyman's cause, was the talk of the town.

Jas was smiling in anticipation even before she began to read it.

The first frame of the comic strip showed Grogan the Cat successfully hailing a taxi. That the taxi drove over his tail in the driver's eagerness for a fare didn't daunt him. The second frame showed Grogan in the back seat of the taxi viewing seventeen different hand-lettered No Smoking signs posted by the driver. The third frame had a crestfallen Grogan reluctantly returning his unlit cigarette to its usual position behind his left ear. The fourth frame depicted the face of the taxi driver, a fat cigar hanging out over his lower lip. The fifth frame showed Grogan becoming asphyxiated by the fumes. The last square had a dizzy-looking Grogan departing the cab. The driver was yelling, ''Have a nice day,'' as the tires were once more about to run over Grogan's tail.

Jas Rafferty considered herself easygoing. She suffered weather forecasts that called for sunny skies and left her caught in downpours with no umbrella. She shrugged off taxi drivers who couldn't speak English and had flunked driver's ed. She accepted with equanimity the fact that any subway car she rode in had at least one of the following: a) a blaring radio; b) a drunk who ended up vomiting on her shoes; or c) a mugger. She deemed it fate that when she was finally able to afford her own apartment and move out of her parents' place, the days of the sexual revolution had come to an end and instead everyone was working out. She felt she must have done something to deserve all the junk mail that came to her and she ended up reading it all out of courtesy. She had learned to expect that the one section of the Sunday newspaper that she was dying to read was going to be the one section missing.

Jas was a New Yorker; she was used to adversity. That was why she felt such an affinity with Grogan the Cat. Every time something unpleasant or unnerving or just plain annoying happened to her, she could be sure that eventually she would be seeing the same thing happen to Grogan. It single-handedly prevented her from becoming paranoid that all the bad things that happened to her in New York were happening to her alone. She guessed that one reason for Grogan's popularity was that misery loved company.

Jas admired the *New York Times*. She knew it was the paper for an intelligent person to buy and read. But the *New York Times* didn't have comic strips, and Jas had grown accustomed to beginning her day with Grogan. She had become addicted to him.

When AT&T was declared a monopoly and people across the nation were besieged with requests to choose their own long-distance telephone company, Grogan parodied their frustration. He was seen receiving a Mailgram from one of the companies. Thinking it was bad news, he suffered a scare. Another company's rates were so confusing to read that all Grogan could figure out was that they had the cheapest rates for calling Afghanistan at 4:20 a.m. A third sent their advertising in an official, government-looking sort of envelope with an Open Immediately demand on the front. When he did, thinking it was his income-tax refund, he was sadly disappointed. Night after night television commercials screamed at him to make a choice—their choice. Grogan finally made his choice, which was to unplug his telephone from the wall and throw it out the window. Thereafter he was seen writing letters rather than making phone calls.

When the subways went on strike, forcing millions of people to find other ways of getting to work, Grogan was seen buying a pair of running shoes. As the strike went on and on and on, Grogan was getting leaner and sleeker and fitter. Grogan could now run up the five flights of stairs in his building without gasping for air. When the subway strike ended and passengers had to pay more money to ride even dirtier subways with even more desperate muggers, Grogan continued walking. As did many of the comic strip's readers, to the consternation of the Transit Authority.

When Grogan's country cousin, Delbert, came to the city to visit, Delbert was seen being lured into a three-card-monte game on Thirty-fourth Street. When he was shown being cheated out of all his money, despite the fact that two uniformed police were in the vicinity, and after Grogan demonstrated just how he had been cheated, the three-card-monte games on Thirty-fourth Street suddenly went underground for a while.

Jas was convinced that Grogan was a help to all those people trying to survive in the city. She knew she needed her fix of Grogan just to get started every day, in the same way coffee drinkers needed their morning fix of caffeine.

Jas was cutting out the Grogan taxi strip and pinning it to her bulletin board when Marlene, the receptionist, buzzed her and told her Stanley wanted to see her in his office.

Jas hoped it was a new case. She also wished that just this once she'd get something interesting, something like the private investigators on TV were always getting. Something with a little adventure to it, a little romance, a little excitement. And, most especially, something that didn't involve using the computer that she still couldn't seem to get the hang of. Leave it to Stanley to computerize the office when the primary reason she worked as a private investigator was that she didn't know how to type well enough to get a position as a secretary, which was a much higher-paying job. Well, no—that wasn't really true. She had always wanted to be a detective. She just hadn't figured on the work requiring a talent for computers.

When Jas walked into Stanley's office, she ignored the straight-backed chair across from his seat and took a seat on the fake-leather couch. The chair faced the window, automatically giving Stanley the advantage while the person facing him was forced to squint just to make out his face. It was one of Stanley's sneaky interrogation techniques.

"I read the interview in 'Our Town,'" said Stanley, which could mean he either hated it or loved it. Stanley had perfected the art of ambiguity.

"Mmm," said Jas, who could be just as ambiguous as Stanley when necessary.

"We've already had calls from two new clients this morning, both of them requesting your services." He was smiling now, but with Stanley a smile could mean anything.

"I see," said Jas, still not discerning the drift of his mood.

"I turned both of them down. It seemed they were more interested in meeting you than in hiring an investigator."

Jas pictured incredibly wonderful men who would have fallen madly in love with her dashing image. TV again. She wished just once they'd have a realistic detective show.

Stanley swerved around in his chair, affording Jas a view of his profile and the elaborate bouffant his hairdresser had created to cover the bald spot on top. "It doesn't hurt for the agency to get some free publicity," he observed, then waited for Jas to speak up.

Jas kept quiet. In her experience of Stanley, positive statements were most often immediately followed by negative statements.

True to form, Stanley said, "Grandstanding, however, usually turns out to be counterproductive."

The time to remain silent was over. When Stanley led the offensive with insults, her defense went into action. "It's a little difficult not to grandstand when you're the only one being interviewed," said Jas. "I mentioned the firm's name three times as per your request." She felt like adding that there wouldn't have been an interview if she hadn't been a personal friend of the interviewer.

Stanley's chair came back around. "When am I going to see some results on the Capetto case?"

"I have surveilled his building at all hours of the day and night. Not once have I seen Mr. Capetto out of his wheelchair."

"We need some evidence, Jas. The insurance company goes to court on it the beginning of next month."

"Stanley, short of dragging him bodily out of his wheelchair and propping him against the side of the building, there is no way I'm going to get a picture of him out of that chair."

"You think he was actually paralyzed?"

"His doctor thinks so. His attorney thinks so. His wife and children appear to think so. I have seen nothing so far to make me think he's a malingerer."

Stanley fiddled with his tie and stroked it as if to soothe it somehow, as if the whole problem would go away if his tie would only calm down. "They're one of our largest accounts," he finally reminded her.

"Does that mean we cheat for them?"

Since Stanley ran his investigative agency along the lines of exaggerated claims, distortion of fact and general deception exceeded only by certain missions to the UN, it meant exactly that. Still, some innate fastidiousness prevented him from spelling it out. He seemed to expect his employees to pick this up through some kind of osmosis. So far, in the interests of supporting herself, Jas had never asked that office policies be spelled out.

"All I ask is that you give it your best," said Stanley, his lie as smooth as any politician's.

"Give it your best" was a new one. Usually he asked for two hundred percent. "You've got it," said Jas, getting up off the couch.

"Sit back down," Stanley said.

Since it sounded like an order rather than a request, Jas resumed her seat.

"We've got a new job," Stanley said. "This is strictly confidential, of course."

"Of course," echoed Jas.

"Kingsley," he said, then paused for the reaction that name would elicit.

"You mean *the* Kingsley? Kingsley Tower and all that?"

Stanley's smile became smug as he appeared to savor the moment.

"Why would they come to us?" Jas asked. "I would think they'd have their own investigators."

"Lawyers, yes; investigators, no. This is a biggie, Jas. If we do well on this, we just might pick them up as a client. Which would be a real coup, if I say so myself. It's going to mean a lot of work and I expect everyone in the office to pitch in and give it their two hundred percent."

That might mean overtime, Jas was thinking. She could use the money, Stanley's salaries being very close to minimum wage.

Stanley's hand went back up to his tie, but this time he was loosening it. This always foreshadowed a lecture. Today being no exception, Stanley cleared his throat and began. "Are you aware, Jas, that there are an estimated two hundred and forty thousand phantom tenants in this city?"

The thought crossed her mind that Stanley had finally lost his marbles. "Are you talking about ghosts, Stanley?"

Stanley shot her an irritated look at being interrupted. "I'm not talking about ghosts; I'm referring to the number of people illegally subletting apartments in rent-controlled or rent-stabilized buildings."

Jas froze. *She* was illegally subletting an apartment. In fact, if she hadn't been given that opportunity, she'd still be living with her parents.

When Stanley saw that he wasn't going to be interrupted again, he continued. "We, of course, are not going after all two hundred and forty thousand of them. We're just going after the ones currently residing in those buildings belonging to Kingsley."

Jas's shell shock subsided. She knew who owned her building and it definitely wasn't Kingsley.

"I'm dividing up the buildings according to areas. Since you live in the Village, you're getting those."

Great. She got to spy on her neighbors.

"I want everyone back here tonight for a special meeting," said Stanley. "That way I'll only have to explain things once. Now get out and start surveilling Capetto again. If you could wrap that up, you'd be able to work full-time on this."

"I'm going over there right now."

"Good. Try to get some results."

The only results she was sure of obtaining were a few more pounds from all the food she consumed while watching Capetto's apartment building from the coffee shop across the street. The only good thing about it was that she could write off the food as expenses.

WHAT STARTED OUT as a mild irritation with the Kingsley Corporation and ended up a full-blown feud began with Harry's reading an ad for a four-day, three-nights package weekend.

In order to live in New York and still preserve his sanity, Harry Keyes spent at least one weekend each month out of the city. The last time he had picked Jamaica as his destination and Kingsley Airlines had been the packager.

On the day of the departure, Harry arrived at JFK at 7:00 a.m., checked his bag, got his boarding pass and was in the departure lounge an hour before take-off, as per the request of the airlines.

Two hours later the passengers were told there would be a twenty-minute delay. There was a certain amount of grumbling by some of the passengers, but most of them were used to airline delays.

Every twenty minutes during the next hour and a half, the same twenty-minute delay was repeated to them over loudspeakers. By then babies were crying, formerly well-behaved children were turning into delinquents, and young couples were falling out of love. Harry, at this point, was still shrugging it off.

At ten-forty-five it was announced that there was a mechanical difficulty on their plane and that another plane had been made available to them. The entire group of people was then herded to another departure gate and, after another delay of twenty-five minutes, finally was able to board the plane.

Once on board, Harry ran into another difficulty. It seemed that the boarding pass for his seat had been issued twice. Since the other man had gotten the seat first, Harry was told that the only empty seat on the plane was at the back, in the smoking section. Harry didn't mind. By this time he was thinking of taking up smoking just for something to pass the time.

After two more hours of sitting on the plane, on the ground, it finally took off. The passengers applauded. Harry was practically comatose from the smoke going up all around him.

When the midafternoon "breakfast" was passed, they ran out of trays when they got to Harry's row. Harry tried to count this as a blessing since he didn't normally like airline food. His growling stomach, however, didn't agree with him.

They arrived over "sun-filled Jamaica" in the middle of a torrential rainstorm and due to poor visibility were forced to circle the airport for two hours. By this time the first day of his four day, three nights was already shot, but Harry wasn't complaining. Just about everyone else on the plane was complaining, but Harry, reading the airline magazine for the third time, was just thankful they had arrived at all.

Two things happened in the airport in Montego Bay. Harry found that his bag was missing, and while he was filling out a claim for it, the limousine to his hotel left without him.

By the time he arrived at his hotel, he didn't even notice that his "king-size" bed was a twin, that the air conditioner didn't work and that a noisy party seemed to be taking place in the next room. He went down to the bar, got quietly drunk on overpriced drinks, then retired for the night.

It rained for the next three days. Each day, when he called the airport regarding his missing luggage, he was told they were tracking it down. By the time he left Jamaica, his bag had still not been found.

When he arrived back in New York it was raining, but everyone assured him the weekend had been perfect.

Harry was still not angry with Kingsley Airlines when he went to their corporate offices on Fifth Avenue to find out where his bag was. He was disappointed in his trip, a little miffed that they couldn't find one bag, but he wasn't really angry.

The Kingsley Building took up one full block on Fifth Avenue. Kingsley's Department Store comprised the first ten floors. Above the store, rising high up into the Manhattan sky, was Kingsley Tower, housing Kingsley Airlines, Kingsley Real Estate Developments, Kingsley Enterprises and all the other businesses owned by Kingsley.

Harry took the glass elevator up to the forty-third floor, where the airlines office was. Here he was told by an unfriendly clerk, who was on the borderline of being out-and-out rude, that they had no record of a claim being filed by him. Still fairly calm, still not giving vent to his temper, which was beginning to manifest itself by a clenching of his teeth, Harry filled out another claim form. And was told, once again, that he would hear from them.

At that point Harry, who knew a runaround when he heard one, figured he could say goodbye to his leather satchel and vacation clothes.

So the weekend wouldn't be a complete loss, Harry had a little fun with it. Through Grogan, he relived the experience, but he didn't mention Kingsley Airlines by name. It wasn't as though he hadn't been given just as bad a time by other well-known airlines. When the comic strip came out and fan mail flooded the *Chronicle*, Harry figured he had hit a responsive chord. Everyone, sooner or later, probably lived through just such an airline fiasco.

A month later, however, he received an envelope in the mail from the Kingsley Corporation. He was sure it was notification that his bag had at last been found. With a pleased smile, he opened the envelope and to his dismay read that Kingsley Real Estate Developments was now the owner of his apartment building, and further, that it was going co-op. Finding out that your building was going co-op was the worst thing that could happen to a resident of New York City. It was worse than being mugged. It was far worse than being lost in Central Park after dark. It was even worse than having your Bloomingdale's charge card revoked. What it meant, in essence, was that if you weren't a millionaire, you'd no longer be living in the city.

The first tiny flicker of something very much like revenge lit deep down in Harry's brain.

JAS GOT BACK to the office on Twenty-third Street just after five and found the meeting about to start. There was Stanley at the head of the conference table; Marlene was on his right with her steno pad in front of her; and ranged around the table were the other five investigators, all of them men. Jas didn't mind being the only woman in the group. This sometimes led to good assignments, such as the time she had had to go undercover in a women's hotel.

Cheap Stanley had even come up with sandwiches and coffee for everyone, which must mean the meeting was going to be lengthy.

"Now that we're all here," said Stanley, with a pointed glance in Jas's direction, "we'll get started. First of all, I want you to think of yourselves as 'lease police.'"

There was an audible groan from Charlie.

"You have a problem with this, Charlie?" Stanley asked.

"Half my friends have illegal sublets," Charlie said, looking around the table for support. Several of the others nodded. Jas stared down at the table, too paranoid about her own illegal sublet even to nod.

Stanley, who owned his own co-op, wasn't sympathetic. "You're all going to get a lot of use out of your computers on this assignment."

This time Jas groaned and several of the men chuckled. More than one of them had tried to explain the P.C.'s workings to her, mostly to no avail. She wished they could go back to the good old days, when the office had a typist they shared.

Stanley was saying something Jas missed, and then Marlene was up and walking around the table, handing thick, stapled stacks of paper to everyone. When Jas got hers, she saw that there was a list of dozens of apartment buildings, all with addresses in the Village, plus lists of the tenants in each building.

"Do we check out everyone in these buildings?" she asked Stanley.

"Everyone," he said. "What you do first is find out whether they have another known address. You should be able to find this out by state income-tax returns and the motor-vehicle department. When there are two addresses, what you want to determine is the primary residence."

"And when we find a suspect?" asked Mervyn.

"Then it's up to your own ingenuity," Stanley answered. "Aside from posing as a government agent or a member of the clergy, both of which are illegal, anything else goes."

Jas was surprised he made that distinction. No doubt Kingsley had said to keep it on the up-and-up.

As though to answer that, Stanley added, "They'll be going to court on these cases, so stay within the letter of the law. When the investigation is done right, the landlords end up winning eighty-five percent of the cases."

Jas didn't like the sound of those odds. Maybe in the course of her investigations she'd hear of an apartment to rent. One that would be legal.

"Cameras?" asked Charlie.

"Definitely," said Stanley.

It sounded as though the questioning would go on forever. Jas finally tuned out, wondering if this job would call for new disguises. She loved disguises. One of the best things about being a private investigator was seeing what creative new ones she could come up with.

AFTER HARRY SPENT most of the day rapping on the doors of the other tenants in his building, a hastily formed tenants' association was formed that night in

Harry's apartment, and Harry found himself elected spokesperson.

Everyone at the meeting was in accord about one thing: no one wanted the building going co-op.

They all had stories of co-op horrors to tell. Everyone had friends or relatives or both who had had terrible experiences; it was happening everywhere.

"The thing is," said Mr. Bernardo from 3F, "they can't legally do anything to get us out until our leases have expired. I don't know about you guys, but I just signed a new three-year lease last month, which means that legally I could hold up the co-op process for a good long time."

"They'll offer us money," said Ms. Dorsky, 6B. "But it won't be enough. It'll just be a token payment, not nearly enough to get into another apartment. If I could even find one. I've lived here thirty-five years. I thought I'd die in this building."

Harry, who had never anticipated dying in the building, also hadn't anticipated its going co-op. He knew he should've, though; it was a sign of the times.

"We aren't the first tenants' association to form over something like this," said Mr. Custodio, 7J. "But the buildings all go co-op eventually. All it does is buy a little time."

"They won't if we stick together on this," said Bernardo. "If none of us decides to take the money and run, if we all hang together, what can they do?"

Custodio disagreed. "Wait. Wait until they turn the water off. Wait until it's winter and we don't have any heat. Wait until they start hassling you on the phone twenty-four hours a day."

Harry said, "First of all, are there any of you who'd prefer to take the money and move?"

One timid young man tentatively lifted his hand in the air. "I was thinking of moving anyway," he said. "I hear you can still find reasonable rents in New Jersey."

"Don't be in a hurry to take their first offer," said Dorsky. "I understand they start low and will go up a few thousand if you don't seem eager."

"Any of the rest of you want to leave?" asked Harry. When no one raised his hand, he said, "Good. Then maybe, with some luck, we can become the first tenants' association to stop a co-op from going through."

"You're looking for a miracle," said a good-looking young woman whom Harry was wondering why he'd never noticed before. That was before he noticed she was holding hands with the good-looking young man seated next to her.

"This Kingsley," said the super, who was going to be out an apartment plus a job. "He's taking over everywhere. He's already got a Kingsley Co-ops East, Kingsley Co-ops West, Kingsley Co-ops North and Kingsley Co-ops South. What's he going to call this one, Kingsley Co-ops Northwest?"

"He lives up in his tower; what does he know of the apartment situation?" said Mr. Neery, 2C.

"Maybe we can put a little pressure on him," said Harry, "if we think it's going to be necessary."

"You can't pressure a guy like Kingsley," said 5A.

"Us putting pressure on Kingsley," Custodio said, "would be like a flea putting pressure on an elephant."

"This kind of thing isn't even news anymore," said the good-looking young man seated next to the good-looking young woman. "If we were the first ones we might be able to pull in some media publicity, but it's old news by now."

"I don't know whether any of you know what I do for a living," said Harry.

No one did, but one of them said, "I hope you're a lawyer."

"Forget lawyers," said Neery. "Let's hope he plays for the Mets. They're the only ones getting any publicity this time of year."

"What position do you play?" asked someone.

"I'm not with the Mets," said Harry, "but I'm a big fan of theirs."

There were a few cheers for the Mets and a few looks of disappointment that he wasn't on the team.

"I write a comic strip that appears in the *Chronicle*," said Harry. "Maybe some of you have seen it. Grogan the Cat?"

There was a hushed silence, then a few smiles, then a chuckle or two, and then, all at the same time, cheers. It would appear Grogan had more fans in the room than the Mets.

"Yeah," said Harry when the cheers had subsided. "Maybe Grogan could be persuaded to take on Kingsley."

"Maybe we're going to get our miracle after all," said 5G.

"Grogan the Cat," said the super, shaking his head in wonder. "If that don't beat all. And here I always thought you were a lazy good-for-nothing who never went out to work."

The super wasn't the only one to think that. All of Harry's friends who had to get up every morning and commute to work thought the same thing.

THE IDEA, LIKE MOST of Harry's good ideas, came to him while he was in the middle of doing something else. The tenants' meeting had broken up and Harry was watching the eleven-o'clock news when inspiration unexpectedly struck.

Going after the morality of throwing long-time tenants out of apartment buildings in order to sell them as co-ops wouldn't do it. He'd already had several strips alluding to the question in the past, and although it was something the readers related to, it hadn't stopped new co-ops from springing up.

No, the only way to get to Kingsley was to hit him where it hurt. And that meant financially. From all he had read about Kingsley, the man was obsessed with making money. And, to date, his biggest money-maker was his department store with various branches around the country and a mail-order-catalog business that had grossed over a billion in sales the previous year.

Harry had never used the comic strip to air a personal grievance before. At least not in a way that might wreak revenge. But he wasn't doing this just for himself. He was doing it for every other tenant in the building, for every dispossessed tenant in the city and those yet to come.

Harry wasn't in the same financial situation as most of the other tenants. He could afford to buy a co-op if he wanted one. He could pay the two hundred and fifty thousand dollars, or whatever ridiculous amount they'd be asking for his ordinary apartment, but what would he get in return for his money? The same apartment, a huge mortgage payment, at least three times his current rent in a monthly maintenance charge, and a bunch of yuppies as his neighbors.

He had been in the same apartment on Eighty-sixth Street for ten years. He'd watched the gradual, creeping changes that had turned what had once been an interesting, multi-ethnic neighborhood into what was now regarded as the trendiest section of the city.

The laundromat that he had always used had been in the same storefront location for over fifty years. Now the high rent had forced it out of business and an art gallery that specialized in neon had taken over and Harry had to commute to another neighborhood to do his laundry. The coffee shops had all given way to eateries with California decor and staggering prices and Harry took to eating breakfast at home. The shoe-repair store had closed down and a wind-sock boutique had taken its place. Harry's shoes still kept needing to be resoled, but he had never felt a need to buy a wind-sock. In fact, he had never even heard of a wind-sock until the store opened and wind-socks were seen blowing in the breeze outside of it. Central Park used to be filled with families on weekends; now it was filled with joggers. The neighborhood deli was now a David's Cookies store. Foreign films had crossed the park and were now to be seen at West Side theaters. The gym was now a health club. The barbershop no longer cut hair; they designed it at four times the price. Shops selling ethnic chic for the home had replaced the real ethnic shopkeepers. But the very lowest blow had occurred when Riley's Bar & Grill,

Harry's longtime hangout, became a health-food store where the only drink you could get was carrot juice.

Someone had to fight back, thought Harry. Someone had to make a stand. And if he wasn't powerful enough, if the tenants' association wasn't powerful enough, if it had to rest on the shoulders of one fat cat, then so be it.

It would be Grogan's finest hour.

Chapter Two

At first no one at Kingsley's Department Store took it very seriously. Most of the employees, in fact, thought it was a riot. The public-relations director for the store had even cut out the comic strip and planned on using it in the weekly newsletter the store put out for its employees. Several people heard him mention that it was great publicity, the kind money couldn't buy.

The comic strip that Monday morning showed Grogan riding up in Kingsley's famous glass elevator and, in case some people didn't recognize the store from that, other passengers in the elevator carried the distinctive Kingsley's shopping bag with the pattern of crowns on it. The last square of the comic strip showed Grogan filling out an application for a Kingsley's charge card.

The rest of the week the comic strip showed Grogan making exorbitant plans concerning all the things he would be able to charge once he got his card. This was pretty funny and Kingsley's employees began taping the strips over their desks or on their cash registers. Some of the sales clerks were swearing that business had picked up as a result.

Even Mr. Kingsley's private secretary thought it was wonderful. She had always hidden the *Chronicle* from her boss, who swore by the *Times*, but now she brought it out in the open and flaunted it. It vindicated her own view of Grogan that, even though he was a street cat, he had a lot of class.

SINCE MORNINGS WERE the only time Jas saw Mr. Capetto being wheeled out of his apartment building, she cut down her surveillance to mornings. That left afternoons and evenings to devote to the Kingsley business.

On the Monday morning when Grogan first entered Kingsley's, a Jas even her mother wouldn't recognize was seated in a booth of the coffee shop facing Mr. Capetto's building, looking at the comic strip for the second time.

In the interests of disguise, of blending into her surroundings, Jas had an all-purpose haircut. Since Mr. Capetto lived on the Lower East Side, her look when she surveilled him was punk. Punk, in that neighborhood, never got a second glance.

Jas thought she had disguise down to a science. Having her hair cut short and always wearing black when on the job was the solution. Right now, for this neighborhood, her brown hair was sticking straight up, thanks to mousse, and she had even sprayed a pink stripe down the center of her scalp. A large safety pin hung from one ear. She had the sleeves of her black cotton sweater rolled up to display the black leather bracelets with silver spikes, and the bottom of her sweater was tucked into her pants with a wide black leather belt around her waist. Her skinny black pants were pushed inside her black boots with the lethal high heels. Her brown eyes were circled with black eyeliner and her lips were a shade of maroon. Despite all this, she was one of the more conservative-looking people in the neighborhood.

All in all, Jas had perfected four looks. There was the punk look, which she was getting pretty tired of. There was the conservative look, which involved curling her hair with a curling iron and wearing subdued makeup, a string of pearls and tasteful flats. There was the look she used for night jobs in bad neighborhoods, which meant no makeup but sometimes a false mustache, running shoes, her hair slicked back and a man's felt hat pulled down low over her face. She hoped she could pass for a boy with this look, but it hadn't yet been put to the test. Then there was her normal look for when she was off the job. This meant her hair combed straight down and hanging a bit shaggily around her face, a little brown mascara and clothes in any color but black. The means for her changes were carried in a large black shoulder bag that never left her sight.

Jas ordered her fourth cup of coffee and wondered at the coincidence of Grogan in Kingsley's at the very same time her agency had taken on Kingsley as a client. It almost seemed like a sign.

It had to be more than just getting a charge card at the store. Grogan's strips always had a point to them, but she couldn't think of any point to that. It was amusing, of course, to see a street cat in a pretentious store like Kingsley's, but the strips usually went beyond amusing. She wondered just what Grogan was up to.

Conversely, she knew exactly what Mr. Capetto was up to when, at exactly ten-thirty, she saw him being wheeled out of the building by Mrs. Capetto. He was going on his daily visit to the nearby park.

And thank God for that daily stroll. Without that, Jas would never get out of the coffee shop.

Jas went up to the cashier to pay her bill.

"Love the pink stripe," he told her. His own hair was dyed to resemble zebra stripes.

"Thanks," said Jas.

"See you tomorrow same time?"

"Probably," said Jas, but hoping this would be her last day in this particular coffee shop. She headed out the door and took off down First Avenue after her quarry.

By now Jas knew exactly what would happen. There would be the uneventful walk to the park. Then, seemingly oblivious of all the drug deals transpiring around them, there would be the walk through the park. Finally, to the north of the park, Mrs. Capetto would leave the wheelchair containing Mr. Capetto beside the steps to the library. She would disappear inside, books under her arm, returning a few minutes later with, Jas supposed, new books. Then they would once again go through the park before returning home.

The only thing that bothered Jas was that the drug dealers now recognized her and sometimes nodded, granting her the status of a regular.

There wasn't much else to do in the park except ride the swings. Jas always availed herself of them while the Capettos were at the library. When the swing was low to the ground, she couldn't see them, but every time it soared into the air, she could. Since this was every other second, she figured that was good enough.

As the Capettos crossed the street to the library, Jas got onto one of the swings. She began pumping her legs, enjoying the wind on her face as the swing rose higher and higher. Then she glanced over to check on Mr. Capetto.

She was so surprised to see something different for a change that her legs automatically stopped pumping. Surrounding Mr. Capetto were three tough-looking boys, probably around sixteen or seventeen. From the looks of things they appeared to be harassing him.

Jas felt that as a good citizen she ought to be doing something about it. As a good investigator, though, she knew she was supposed to stay out of it. Any involvement with the quarry was likely to blow her cover.

Suddenly her swing had lost its momentum and she was too low to see over the shrubbery. She jumped off the swing and ran over to hide behind the bushes and see what was happening. She could see the frustrated look on Mr. Capetto's face as one of the boys grabbed his hat and the paralyzed man couldn't do anything about it.

She hated herself for not trying to stop it. She rationalized that it was only a hat, but then she saw another of the boys start to rock the wheelchair. She was just about to shout at them to stop when she saw the most surprising thing of all. Mr. Capetto was suddenly jumping out of his chair and waving his fists in the air.

Jas was too stunned to react for a moment. She had been certain Mr. Capetto was actually paralyzed. Then, belatedly remembering why she was there, she reached into her bag for her camera, hoping he'd still be out of the wheelchair so that she could get it on film.

It was beautiful. Not only did she get a shot of Mr. Capetto out of the wheelchair, but he was several feet away from it and punching one of the boys.

It was turning out to be one of her best days yet. She'd never have to sit in that coffee shop again. She'd never have to dress punk again, or at least not for a while. And she had saved another case for Paragon Investigations.

The only sour note would be Stanley. Stanley was going to say, "I told you so." She really hated it when Stanley said that.

THE NEXT WEEK the Grogan the Cat comic strips were also funny, but not for Grogan. A sadly disappointed cat was refused a charge card. No reason was given. The discriminated-against cat was seen slinking around the city like an outcast, his tail between his legs.

The sales clerks in Kingsley's were finding it very entertaining when customers would jokingly ask them why Grogan was being refused credit. The sales manager of Kingsley's was heard to have made a joke about Grogan at the weekly sales meetings.

The weekend street vendors outside of Kingsley's began selling Grogan T-shirts and buttons, both of them printed with the words: Give Grogan a Charge Account.

Most of the employees working that weekend ran outside on their breaks and bought either buttons or T-shirts. When one of the stock clerks tried wearing his new T-shirt on the job, however, his supervisor made him remove it. This bit of gossip made the rounds and everyone laughed about it.

HARRY'S tenants' association held a Grogan party.

SINCE HER CAPETTO SUCCESS, Jas was working full-time on the Kingsley case. At first it was just boring office work. She had to look up every tenant to see if she or he had filed New York City income-tax statements. If not, they were suspect.

The long list she finally had of these suspects then had to be checked again with the motor-vehicle bureau. Those who had driver's licenses also had addresses of record, and these were also listed by Jas. If the addresses didn't coincide with the Manhattan addresses she had, these names were starred.

There were other ways of checking and cross-checking, and Jas did them all. It was tedious work and her eyes got bloodshot from sitting in front of her computer, but she couldn't charge Stanley with discrimination because all the men were doing exactly the same work. Even Stanley wasn't taking two-hour lunches anymore. The whole agency was putting out its two hundred percent for Kingsley.

Everything Jas did on the job was confidential, but she nonetheless confided in Arnie. Arnie was her best friend. Arnie heard every detail of every aborted romance Jas went through. He also heard about all her cases.

On the same Sunday that the vendors were doing a brisk business selling Grogan T-shirts outside of Kingsley's, Jas and Arnie were sitting out on the front stoop of their building on Christopher Street off Hudson. They were next-door neighbors as well as best friends.

As Jas was relating to him the details of her new case, Arnie's eyes began to glaze over. This was unusual; usually they looked avid when she was discussing work. "What's wrong?" she asked him.

"Nothing," mumbled Arnie.

"Don't tell me 'nothing'; you're turning white."

"Can you keep a secret, Jas?"

"Of course I can. I tell you all my secrets, don't I?"

"I'm serious."

"I tell you everything, and you won't tell me one lousy secret?"

Arnie's eyes darted around to see if anyone was around to overhear him. Then he whispered, "This is different; this is serious business, Jas."

"In about one minute, Arnie, I'm going to knock you off the stoop."

"I'm one of those phantom tenants."

Jas's mouth dropped open.

Arnie gave her a wild-eyed look. "I knew I shouldn't have told you."

Jas put her arm around his shoulders. "Arnie, it's okay."

"That's easy for you to say."

"If it makes you feel any better, so am I."

"You?"

Jas nodded.

"Somehow that doesn't make me feel any better. I figured if I was caught, I could move in with you."

"It's not just us. There are two hundred and forty thousand of us in the city."

"No wonder New Yorkers are paranoid."

Jas nodded. "At least Kingsley doesn't own our building."

"Yeah, but he's probably not the only one doing this. Maybe at this very moment someone is investigating us."

"It could be worse," said Jas.

"Worse? How could it be worse?"

"Our building could go co-op."

"That's what the guy who's subletting to me is waiting for," said Arnie. "He thinks he'll make a killing when it does. What about you? Who are you subletting from?"

"An aunt. She lived in this building for years."

"I don't think that's illegal," said Arnie. "I think it's okay to let a member of the family live in it."

"She's dead," said Jas.

"Oh."

"She wasn't dead when she sublet to me. She was in the hospital. I just never reported it to the owners of the building."

"I don't blame you."

"I couldn't find another apartment I could afford. I really looked, Arnie. I looked for two years; it was almost a full-time occupation. I'm almost thirty. I couldn't face living with my parents any longer."

"It's a strange world, Jas. Here we are, both of us living in one-room apartments that aren't much bigger than prison cells. We share that space with colonies of expatriate roaches of German origin and the occasional mouse. If you're anything like me, you never complain about a lack of heat or hot water because you don't want to be noticed since you're illegally subletting. And despite all that, we consider ourselves lucky because we have an apartment at all. If we lived in any other city, they wouldn't be able to pay us to live in dumps like that.''

"I hear you can get a three-room apartment in Hoboken for under a thousand a month."

"Yeah, but who wants to live in Hoboken?"

"I feel guilty as hell about what I'm doing, Arnie."

"I've learned to live with it."

"I don't mean the apartment. I mean my job. I'm going to be responsible for people like us getting thrown out of their apartments."

"Then quit."

"And do what? That was the only agency that would hire me."

"Open your own office."

"Arnie, I have exactly seventy-two dollars in the bank, and I won't have that after I pay my phone bill. And I can't work out of my apartment because I'm not there legally. Anyway, I like my job usually."

"If you're going to do it, I have a great idea for you."

"I could use a great idea. The paperwork is done, but I haven't come up with the next step."

"That's what I'm talking about. What you need is documented evidence, right?"

"Right. Like pictures of the people going in and out of the apartment."

"I've got a better idea. I do it all day long, myself."

Jas couldn't figure out what Arnie did as an employee of the To-and-Fro Messenger Service that would be helpful to her.

"I'll even loan you one of my bikes," said Arnie.

"I'm supposed to pose as a messenger while I take their pictures?"

"Nope. Better than that. What you do is deliver a phony envelope to them that requires their signature. Then, when the occupant of the apartment in question signs for it, you compare the name and signature to the one on the lease."

"What a devious mind you have, Arnie. Now you're going to have me paranoid if I ever get an envelope delivered to me."

"Just sign your aunt's name, that's all."

"I wouldn't have to wear black," said Jas. "I could dress like a regular person in jeans and a sweat shirt."

"And a baseball cap," said Arnie. "Messengers always wear baseball caps. And a backpack."

"It'll be fun riding a bike. But what exactly do I get them to sign?"

"Don't worry. I'll get you all the forms you'll need. You'll just have to provide the envelopes."

"Arnie, you're a genius."

"I know."

THE THIRD WEEK into the Tenants' Association vs Kingsley's campaign, things became more serious. Grogan began his own campaign directed at getting himself a charge card. He suggested to all the readers who had Kingsley's cards that they cut them up in little pieces and either mail them to the store or drop them off in person.

Thousands of Kingsley's charge cards, duly cut to pieces, were received in the mail that week at both the flagship stores in Manhattan and branch stores all over the country. Moreover, thousands of people walked into the stores, availed themselves of the nearest counter and dumped their little pieces of charge cards all over Kingsley's clean counters.

Things got worse. The Manhattan store, which usually did a very brisk lunch-hour business, now was being picketed by secretaries on their lunch hour carrying signs aloft with pictures of Grogan on them. Give The Cat a Break read some of the signs. Don't Shop Where Grogan Isn't Wanted read others.

The store, once the busiest in the city, began to resemble a library. It was very quiet and very few people were coming through the revolving doors.

The sales clerks, who had enjoyed their brief moment of popularity, now found themselves as unpopular as deposed dictators.

The president began to take it very seriously when sales dropped to an unprecedented low.

The war had begun.

HARRY GOT A CALL from his boss at Press Syndicate in St. Louis. Harry thought he'd gone too far this time, that Bob was calling him to fire him.

Instead, Bob said, "Love it, Harry. Circulation was up this week on every newspaper featuring Grogan and sales in New York are out of sight. Plus a couple of dozen other papers have picked up your strip."

"I thought you might be afraid of a lawsuit," said Harry, to whom the thought had occurred more than once.

"Not to worry," said Bob. "I was told to assure you that if Kingsley brings one against you personally, Press Syndicate will cover any costs."

"I appreciate your support, Bob."

"Listen, no one likes Floyd Kingsley. Particularly no one in St. Louis. You know what he's out to buy now? The Cardinals. And he wants to move them to Canada. Don't worry, Harry—everyone here is behind you three hundred percent."

JAS, IN HER ROLE as messenger, was having four times the success of any of the other investigators.

Once in a while, of course, her ruse didn't work. One young man blatantly signed the name "Mrs. Rosalie Wilson" on the dotted line, but most of them signed their real names and thus also signed their fate.

She was so successful, in fact, that Stanley had her give a seminar to the other investigators to teach them just what it was she was doing right and they were doing wrong.

"You're not getting me on any bicycle," said Charlie, who weighed in at a little over two hundred and seventy pounds.

"Not all messengers ride bicycles," Jas said.

"I like it," said Mervyn. "It beats taking pictures of them. A couple of guys tried to punch me out when I took their pictures. Also, the evidence will stand up in court better. A picture could be of a friend visiting, but someone signing for something as the occupant is something else."

"She's a regular ball of fire, isn't she?" asked Stanley. That was his highest accolade.

ALL WAS NOT CALM in the penthouse suite of Kingsley Tower.

Floyd "The King" Kingsley, who had Charlie beat by about fifty pounds, wasn't taking it sitting down.

He struggled up out of his chair, waved his Havana cigar in the air and sprayed spittle a good three feet when he roared out, "Who the hell is responsible for this?"

His minions drew in a collective breath as each waited for the other to speak.

It was King's nephew, Teddy, who finally summoned up the courage. "His name is Harry Keyes, King."

"And who in hell is Harry Keyes?"

"He's the creator of Grogan."

"I could figure that one out for myself. What I'd like to know is, why's he going after me?"

"Not you personally, sir. It's the store he's going after."

"Well, forgive me for taking it personally, Teddy, but it does happen to be my store."

"I don't know, King. We've checked our records and he's never applied for or been turned down for a charge card with us."

"Do you have a phone number for him?" asked King.

Teddy nodded.

"Then what in hell are you waiting for? Get him on the line for me." There were times, albeit few, when

King felt he had to personally go to the people. Those times always involved money.

Teddy took a tentative step toward King's desk and reached for the phone. He got an outside line, then punched in the number in question. He heard the phone being picked up and then someone said hello.

"Mr. Harry Keyes," said Teddy.

"Speaking."

"Mr. Kingsley would like to speak to you."

"It's about time," heard the King as he put the receiver to his ear.

"You seem to have a personal vendetta going against me, Mr. Keyes," said the King in an affable tone of voice.

"Not entirely personal," said Harry.

The affable tone turned to one of steel. "I want it stopped."

"That could be arranged," said Harry.

"I was sure it could."

"As the spokesperson for the 80 West Eighty-sixth Street Tenants' Association, we would certainly take kindly to the idea of your not going through with your plans for our building's going co-op."

King, who had never seen a building that he didn't immediately visualize as a co-op, choked on his cigar. "This sounds like blackmail," he sputtered.

"I suppose it does," said Harry.

"Nobody blackmails the King," roared Kingsley, then slammed down the phone in Harry's ear.

Hooded eyes turned in Teddy's direction. "That detective agency we hired to go after the phantom tenants—"

"Paragon," said Teddy.

"Get them on the phone."

JAS, FEELING TOTALLY out of place in the luxurious surroundings dressed in her messenger disguise, stood in front of Mr. Kingsley's desk as his eyes took in every aspect of her appearance.

Two could play at that game, and Jas did. His body looked as though it had never been exercised; his skin looked as though it had never been touched by the sun; his pin-striped suit looked custom-made. His clean-shaven face resembled that of a particularly fat baby: his cheeks were round, his mouth a moist rosebud, and the soft curls that tumbled over his forehead had the fine-textured look of an infant's hair. His nose was pert. He didn't look like a particularly nice baby, though. He looked like the kind of baby who was about to open his mouth and start screaming nonstop for his pacifier. And behind his baby-blue eyes lurked an unnerving look of intelligence.

He spoke first, and his face, when not in repose, lost its infantile aspect. "So you're the hotshot detective, huh?"

"Private investigator," she corrected him. Even if she hadn't disliked everything she'd ever heard about him, she would have hated him on sight. She got the feeling that he fancied himself a modern-day Henry VIII, only with a cigar rather than a scepter in his hand.

"You can sit down, hotshot."

Jas's blood pressure rose a few points. He sounded every bit as obnoxious as he looked. She sat down, saying as she did so, "Oh, how kind of you."

Kingsley shot her a suspicious look. "How'd a nice girl like you get to be a detective?"

"I'm not all that nice," said Jas.

"Good. Because this is no job for a namby-pamby."

He seemed to be waiting for a reply, but Jas, used to Stanley's tactics, waited him out.

Kingsley handed her a piece of paper with a name and address written on it. "Get him."

"How do you mean?"

"I mean any way you can. First find out if he's a phantom tenant. If he's not, I want some dirt on him. If it's criminal, excellent. If not, anything embarrassing will do."

"I'll try, sir."

"That's not good enough. Just do it. And keep in mind that time is of the essence."

"What if he's clean?"

"It's been my experience that nobody's clean," said Kingsley.

That had rather been Jas's experience, too, but she hated the idea of sharing the same views with Kingsley.

"Job too difficult for you?" asked Kingsley.

"Not at all," Jas assured him.

"Then get on it."

As Jas turned to go, Kingsley said, "And, hotshot, we don't accept failure around here."

Jas felt benevolent in allowing him the last word.

During her trip down in the glass elevator, she wondered who Harry Keyes was. Whoever he was, she felt sorry for him.

Chapter Three

When Jas left the Kingsley offices, she felt she had two choices. She could go back to the office and make use of her computer to find out whether Harry Keyes was a phantom tenant. Or she could go straight up to the address in question, posing as a messenger, and see if the signature she obtained corresponded with the name of the tenant of record.

Because she hated anything having to do with the computer, she opted for the second.

It was a beautiful day in late September. The temperature was in the seventies, the humidity was low, and while the weather forecast had said partly cloudy, Jas couldn't find a cloud anywhere.

Although she had found Mr. Kingsley obnoxious, generally speaking things were going well for her. She was currently considered the star investigator by Stanley, she was making enough overtime that she was hopeful of being able to pay off her detective-school loan this month, and she got out of the Kingsley Building just in time to prevent a thief from stealing the seat off Arnie's bike.

She rode up Sixth Avenue to Fifty-ninth Street, then headed for Central Park West. The ride alongside the park was delightful. The leaves on the trees were turning to Halloween colors—half were still orange and the other half were already black from the soot—and everyone seemed to be out riding their bikes. She thought that after she got the tenant's signature she'd play hooky from work for a couple of hours and peddle through the park.

When she got to the address of the building she was looking for on Eighty-sixth Street, she locked the bike to a streetlight and headed for the door. Inside the foyer she saw a sign that looked new, announcing that the building was now the possession of Kingsley. It was exactly the kind of sign she hoped never to see in her own building.

She found the buzzer for 6A and noted that no name was in the slot under it. This could be an indication that he was a phantom tenant. On the other hand, she had a name under her own buzzer, although the name belonged to her aunt.

She pressed the buzzer and a few moments later a static-charged voice came out of the intercom, asking who she was.

"Aim-To-Please Messenger Service," she said into the speaker.

The buzzer sounded to unlock the inside door, and she pushed it open and headed for the elevators. Signs on both of them said that they were out of order.

Running up the first flight of stairs was a snap. All the cycling she'd been doing must have strengthened her leg muscles. Running up the second, third and fourth flights got progressively worse. She thought of making a report to Kingsley that the elevators in one of his buildings weren't working.

The last flight was a killer. She had seen many detective shows where the detective raced up stairs, usually with gun drawn, burst through doors, jumped across roofs, etcetera. Except they were actors and had stunt men. Right now she could use a stunt man.

When she reached the top she fell forward on her knees. She felt like a contender in the New York Marathon. No, she felt worse. She felt close to death.

The door across the landing opened and an extremely appealing man stood there looking down at her. He was barefoot, wearing jeans and a T-shirt that said I Love Jamaica. The T-shirt looked new.

"You walked all the way up here?" he asked her.

Jas nodded as she pulled herself to her feet. Her legs felt ready to cave in. At this level she could see that his eyes behind his wire-rimmed glasses were green. Actually, his hair was also green, as was his skin. No doubt because she was viewing them from behind green-tinted sunglasses.

"You're the first messenger who's ever walked all the way up. Usually they make me go down."

"We aim to please," said Jas, rather liking that touch. She had made up the name of the fictitious messenger service herself.

He leaned against the door and grinned at her. He had the kind of smile that curved his mouth up, rather like a happy-face drawing. It was a great smile. "You like being a messenger?" he asked her.

"When it's not raining."

"You ride a bike?"

She nodded. She wished he wouldn't be so friendly; it was really making her feel guilty.

"It's kind of dangerous, isn't it? I always see messengers weaving in and out of the traffic."

"I haven't been hit yet," Jas said. "Not that the taxis don't try."

She handed him the manila envelope with the form on top of it. "Please sign," she said. The guy was sure going to be surprised when he found that she had stuffed the envelope with several Grogan comics so that it wouldn't appear empty.

He was signing his name as he said, "This is great. I was waiting for this."

Jas didn't like the sound of that. It sounded as though there was another messenger right on her heels.

When he handed it back to her, she checked the name. He was either very cunning or he was actually Harry Keyes. Then she saw that he was still standing there and was starting to rip open the envelope. With a hasty "Have an interesting day, sir," she fled down the stairs, hoping that her legs wouldn't give out before she reached the street.

As she sped away she wondered what Mr. Keyes thought of the comics she had enclosed for his viewing pleasure.

HARRY WAS ALREADY PICTURING Grogan as a messenger, his tail flying out behind his bike. Then he pulled out what was inside the envelope and wondered why his accountant had messengered over copies of his old strips. As far as he knew, George didn't have a sense of humor.

KING CALLED TEDDY into his office. It was five
o'clock and King was bored. Five o'clock meant his
employees would be going home, leaving him all alone
in his penthouse with nothing to do but order his servants around. Ordering servants around had lost its
novelty value a long time ago.

Teddy would no doubt stay after five o'clock with
no complaints. He didn't dare complain—not when he
was owned by King.

In the office safe was a contract saying that Teddy
owed King eighty-six thousand dollars for his college
education and two hundred and forty thousand dollars for his co-op apartment on East Eighty-first
Street. In effect, the contract said that Teddy would
work for King until such personal loans, plus eighteen percent interest, were paid off. At the salary King
paid Teddy, he figured he had Teddy indentured to
him for life.

"Yes, sir?" said Teddy, taking his usual place,
which meant standing in front of King's desk.

"That private detective who was in here," said
King.

"Yes. That would be Jas Rafferty."

"Odd name, Jas."

"Indeed."

"I want her investigated."

Teddy looked nonplussed. "You want to investigate an investigator?"

"Are you questioning my order, Teddy?"

"No, sir, not at all. I was just getting it straight in
my mind, sir."

"I want to know everything about her."

"Yes, sir. I suppose you don't want Paragon doing the investigating."

"That's a logical supposition, Teddy; you deserve high marks on that."

Teddy swelled with pride. "Thank you, sir."

King loved reading detectives' reports. It was rather like having a friend who confided in him, but, unlike having a real friend, he didn't have to do any confiding in return.

JAS WAS TREATING ARNIE to dinner at the Key Café on Hudson. Usually the place would be beyond her means, but she was making overtime and figured she owed Arnie.

She had just finished telling Arnie about her latest messenger run, ending with, "I'm in real trouble, Arnie. He checked out."

"So now you have to get some dirt on him, huh?"

"I don't want to do it. I sort of liked him."

"For you, 'sort of' liking him are pretty strong words."

"He was cute."

"Cute doesn't tell me anything."

Jas thought a moment. "He looked like a young John Denver. Before he started wearing contacts."

"I never liked his music much," said Arnie.

"I don't like his music, either. I'm just saying that this guy looks like him. He just doesn't look like the type who's into the kind of shady dealings Kingsley would be interested in hearing about."

"What'd you think of Kingsley?"

"Gross."

"You mean the way he looked or the way he acted?"

"Both. He's really disgusting, Arnie. Why is it that it's never the nice people who hire investigators?"

"It's a dirty business, Jas."

"I guess."

"And you love it."

She smiled. "You're right, I do. Nice people all the time would get real dull."

"So what're you going to do next?"

"I'm planning on having dessert. Probably the key-lime mousse. How about you?"

"Sounds good to me."

"But to answer your question, I suppose I'll have to search his apartment."

"You private eyes lead such exciting lives."

"You're going to get to share in some of that excitement, Arnie. Those pictures I took of Capetto are supposed to be ready tonight. Come by with me to pick them up and I'll let you have one of them as a souvenir."

"I'll settle for the key-lime mousse."

THE UPPER WEST SIDE being the heart of yuppie-dom, Jas required a special disguise. She had noticed that most of the yuppies had looked as though they were on their way to a safari, the clothes no doubt purchased at the Banana Republic that had opened on Broadway.

Jas didn't buy her clothes at the Banana Republic, but she figured khaki pants, a white cotton sweater, running shoes and curly hair would suffice. That and her imitation diving watch.

So disguised, she set off on the IRT subway the next day for a little extracurricular breaking and entering. They had been her favorite subjects at detective school and she'd had few opportunities to put those skills to work.

Jas instantly blended into the crowd as she sauntered up Columbus Avenue. She was feeling confident and in control of the situation and enjoying her status as Stanley's hotshot. She would discover infamous secrets craftily hidden away in Mr. Keyes's apartment, save the day for Mr. Kingsley and, perhaps, get a nice juicy bonus from Stanley.

But she still wished Mr. Keyes hadn't been so appealing.

She casually entered the foyer of his building and pressed the buzzer. This was the first thing they taught you in the breaking-and-entering class. You were never, ever, to assume the quarry wasn't at home.

She waited an impatient five minutes and pressed the buzzer once again. Three minutes later she inserted her bank card between the door and the door frame and let herself into the lobby of the building. Unfortunately, the elevators were still out of order.

This time Jas paced herself. As soon as she reached a landing, she rested for thirty seconds before ascending the next flight of stairs. Thus, when she reached the sixth floor, she was only slightly winded.

Taking no unnecessary chances, she knocked at the door of 6A and then waited an additional five minutes before taking out the tools that were sometimes referred to as "burglar" tools but that she preferred thinking of as "investigator" tools.

The first two locks were a piece of cake. The third was slightly more difficult but not impossible. She quietly pushed open the door and just as quietly closed it behind her.

The second thing she had been taught in the breaking-and-entering class was to look for another way out in case the occupant returned unexpectedly. With this in mind, she headed down the hall to the large room with the windows. Any escape would necessarily have to be out of a window.

Halfway across the nicely polished wood floors of the room she came to a halt. She wasn't looking at all the books in the bookshelves or the colorful graphics on the walls. The comfortable furniture in primary colors barely caught her attention. What did was the white Formica drawing table with the cartoon strip of Grogan in progress.

Now her attention was drawn to the rest of the room and she couldn't help noticing the profusion of Grogan memorabilia wherever she looked. In fact, settled comfortably in a rocking chair was what could be the prototype of Grogan, an enormous black-and-white cat with what resembled a lopsided black mustache. The cat didn't even open his eyes.

Jas found it impossible to suppose that anyone who loved Grogan as much as Mr. Keyes presumably loved Grogan could have anything of a sleazy nature to hide.

She walked over to the drawing table and took a closer look at the work in progress. And there it was, in the corner of one of the strips that was finished— the initials H.K., which she had never really noticed before. Or perhaps she had, but it hadn't registered.

It began to make sense. Harry Keyes wasn't just a potential phantom tenant whom Mr. Kingsley wanted to evict. Harry Keyes was the man behind the cat who was currently giving Kingsley's Department Store such a hazing.

And she was being paid to be on the wrong side!

As she was availing herself of a look at a future comic strip, the apartment suddenly became very quiet. It was then that she realized that what she had taken for the muted noise of traffic from the street had actually been the sound of a shower. And if the shower was located in this apartment, there was a strong possibility that Mr. Keyes was at home.

She turned and started for the door but she hadn't gotten two feet when she heard a sound from that direction. Heart pounding, she rushed to one of the windows that was open a couple of inches and shoved it open all the way.

She had been hoping to find a fire escape. Instead, there was a minute balcony, and she quickly climbed out the window and closed it after her.

The balcony, however, was no solution. As soon as Mr. Keyes walked into the living room and looked out the window she would be fully in his sight. And if he called the cops and Stanley had to bail her out of jail, the hotshot of the office would no doubt find herself out of a job.

She looked around and saw a ledge about ten inches wide jutting out from the building. It might be possible for her to ease herself the length of the ledge and, when she got to the end, jump down to the roof of the next building. Of course it also might not be possible, but she didn't even want to think about that. And, luckily for her, she had no phobia about heights.

On the other hand, she wasn't the most graceful person in the world.

HARRY WAS JUST PUTTING the finishing touches on the strip when he thought he heard what sounded like chanting coming from the street.

Curious, he walked over to the window and opened it up. The balcony obstructed part of his view, but still he could see a multitude of schoolchildren, and what they appeared to be chanting was, "Jump, jump, jump!"

Harry climbed out on the balcony to get a better view and that's when he saw the yuppie on the ledge. He had never before seen a person in the process of committing suicide and it scared the hell out of him.

"Don't listen to them," he said, in what he hoped was a calm voice. He certainly didn't want to startle her.

The woman turned her head so that her face was fully in his view, and the weird thing was she looked familiar. At the same time, he was sure he didn't know her. "Please don't jump," he said. "Just hang in there and I'll call the police. And maybe the fire department."

Her eyes became very wide. "Please don't call the police."

He took this to mean she preferred the fire department and he was climbing back in the window to call them when she said, "Don't call anyone."

He was one leg in the window and one out when he turned his head to look at her. "They'll get someone who knows how to talk you down. I don't think I'd be very good at that."

Grogan materialized on the windowsill and began rubbing against Harry. Harry was reaching around to shove the cat back inside when the woman said, "I've never had a fear of heights, but when the kids started shouting I looked down and now I can't seem to move."

Well, that sounded all right. If she couldn't move, then she wasn't going to jump. "You want to talk about it?" asked Harry.

She appeared to be giving that some serious consideration. "Not really," she said at last.

Harry very slowly pulled his leg through the window and leaned against the side of the balcony facing her. He was careful not to make any sudden moves. New Yorkers tended to get jumpy when people made sudden moves, and getting jumpy where she was standing could be deadly. "Okay, I realize I'm a stranger and you probably don't want to talk to me, but I've got a friend who's an astro-shrink and he might be able to help you. You want me to call him?"

"When're you going to jump, lady?" came a challenging voice from the street, but the woman ignored it. Harry felt like going down and shoving a fist down the kid's throat.

"What's an astro-shrink?" she wanted to know.

"He does analysis by the stars. He's a good friend of mine. I've never actually had a session with him, but he's got a lot of clients who swear by him."

"I don't believe in astrology."

"I don't, either," said Harry. He didn't believe much in psychology, either, but right now he wished he had a little more knowledge along those lines. "How about a priest? You want to talk to a priest?"

"I'm not Catholic."

"I'm not, either," said Harry. "What about your hairdresser?"

"My what?"

"Your hairdresser. I hear women always talk to their hairdressers."

"I cut it myself."

"Really?" said Harry. "I've been doing the same thing lately. Since they started calling it styling, it's kind of put me off." He looked down and saw that some of the children were getting bored and leaving. "How about your mother? You want me to give her a call?"

"God, no," said the woman. "She'd kill me if she knew I was up here."

"Sounds like my mother," said Harry. It was beginning to seem as though they had a lot in common. It was just that he didn't know whether he wanted to have a lot in common with someone who felt impelled to jump off a building.

"Well, I don't know who else to suggest. Have you got any ideas?"

"I'd just as soon you didn't call anybody. I was hoping this would be a private moment."

Harry looked down at the street. "Well, you seem to have attracted a crowd."

"Bad timing. I guess school just let out."

"Well, I know you'd probably like me to leave, but I just wouldn't feel right about it."

"You can stay; I don't mind."

"Look," he said, "my name is Harry. What's yours?"

"Jas."

"Like 'all that jazz'?"

She shook her head. "No, like Jasmine."

"Well, listen, Jas, could I get you something to drink? I imagine a person could get thirsty standing out there."

"No, thanks, but could I use your bathroom?"

"You'd have to come in to do that."

"I realize that," said Jas. "Maybe if you held out your hand I could grab hold of it. I'd feel a lot better if I was holding on to something."

Feeling greatly relieved, Harry leaned over the side of the balcony and held out his hand. When she took it, he managed a firm grasp on hers and said, "Take it slowly, now. There's no hurry."

As she sidestepped over to the balcony, the kids could be heard booing this new development. Harry wondered if the violence on TV had anything to do with it or whether kids were just naturally blood-thirsty.

When she was standing on the railing, Harry put his free hand on her waist and hoisted her down. She weighed practically nothing. "I'm afraid you're going to have to climb in the window," he said, pointing out the way and letting her go first.

Once inside, he said, "The bathroom's down the hall and to your left. Are you sure you wouldn't like something to drink?" He had in mind coffee, tea, maybe a Coke. He hoped she wasn't into things like carrot juice.

She said, "Have you got any gin?"

"I'm pretty sure I do. What would you like in it?"

"Ice cubes," she said, then disappeared down the hall.

Harry thought it seemed a little early to start drinking, but she probably needed something to calm her down. And maybe the gin would loosen her tongue enough so that she'd tell him what it was that had brought her to the edge of suicide. He knew it was pretty nasty of him, but he was already visualizing Grogan talking someone off a ledge. He'd make it funny, of course, not like the real thing.

Actually, he wasn't sure he ought to listen to her story. He was a sucker for sad stories, particularly from women. Living on the West Side, he had met his share of aspiring actresses over the years. As soon as he'd meet one and hear about all the hassles an actress had to go through, from being judged and rejected at cattle calls to fighting off the assistant directors, he would immediately get this strong protective instinct and want to take her away from it all. Actresses, however, never wanted to be taken away from it all. Actresses wanted to star on Broadway, or at least on *All My Children*.

And if it wasn't an actress, it was your normal, everyday working woman in the city, the kind who had been dumped on by so many men that she no longer believed anything any man had to say to her. This also brought out his protective instincts, and also the wish to prove that not all men were rats, that there were a few decent men left in New York. And again he would want to take these women away from it all, but they didn't want to be taken away from it all, either. They wanted successful careers. And most of them had become just as proficient as the men when it came to dumping on someone.

But he couldn't help the way he was feeling. Here was a woman—a quite appealing woman even if she were a yuppie—who had actually attempted to end it all. His protective instincts were out in full force. Like Grogan, he aspired to right all wrongs.

When she came back he had a gin for her and a beer for himself and he was sitting at his drawing table. He handed her the drink and waved her to the couch. Instead of following his directions, though, she looked down at the strip he had just finished. It brought a smile to her face, which he was sure was a good sign.

"You're not the person who does those, are you?" she asked.

"Guilty," said Harry.

"He's my favorite," said Jas. "And he looks just like your cat."

If she liked Grogan, she had to like him, didn't she? After all, Grogan was just a figment of his imagination. "Wrong," said Harry. "The drawing looks just like the real Grogan."

"I love the way you've gone after Kingsley's. I'm not sure what the point of it is, but I never did like that store."

She really was a woman after his own heart. "I'm afraid you'll have to wait to find out what the point of it is."

She wandered over to his bookshelves and tilted her head to read the titles. Harry was glad his guide to picking up women in New York wasn't in full view. Not that he'd ever actually put the suggestions to the test. Things like taking a course in cooking with a wok and hanging out on the third floor of Bloomingdale's hadn't appealed to him.

On the other hand, if the book had suggested picking up a woman who was perched on a ledge waiting to jump, he would've thought the author was crazy. And yet here he was having a drink with her in his own apartment.

"I swear this isn't a line," said Harry, "but haven't I seen you someplace before?"

She shrugged. "I suppose it's possible."

"You look familiar but I can't place you."

"I'm always reminding people of someone else."

It was something about her, but he couldn't quite get a fix on it. He knew as long as he was concentrating on it, though, it wouldn't come. "I hope it wasn't a guy."

She turned to look at him. "I remind you of a guy?"

"I meant I hope it wasn't something some guy did to you that made you want to jump."

Her mouth opened and then closed. The lips took on a stubborn look.

"I guess it's none of my business." Of course it was his ledge she just happened to pick.

"It was a lot of things," Jas said, slowly crossing the room to sit on the couch. She took a long sip of the gin and then settled back. Grogan, obviously miffed at the company, jumped off the couch and headed for the bedroom. "I lost my job, then I had my purse snatched on the subway, and yesterday I found out my building's going co-op."

Losing her job—well, he guessed that could be traumatic but certainly not worth ending her life over.

And having her purse snatched must be a fairly regular occurrence in the city. But her building's going co-op—he could understand suicidal feelings over something like that. And if not suicidal, at least murderous. "I know what you mean, Jas. My building's going co-op, too. What you need to do is form a tenants' association and try to fight it."

"That's like trying to fight city hall."

"Maybe, but I refuse to go down without a fight." She didn't seem impressed or even interested, so he said, "What kind of work do you do?"

"Do you know anything about computers?"

Harry shook his head.

"I'm a computer programmer."

"I thought they were in great demand. I imagine you'll find another job easily enough."

"It's not that easy; everyone's into computers these days."

"Not me," said Harry.

"They've got the kind you can draw on now. You could probably use one to do your comic strip."

"I guess I'm not the high-tech type."

Jas finished off the gin and stood up. "You've been very kind, Harry, but I better go."

Harry was reluctant to see her go so soon. For all he knew, she might be headed for another building to jump off of. "I'll walk with you—which way are you headed?"

"I was thinking of going to the movies."

Harry loved movies. "Which one?"

"There's a theater in Times Square that's having a Bruce Lee festival, three of his movies. If I'm depressed, Bruce Lee movies really cheer me up."

"I love Bruce Lee movies," said Harry, which was an out-and-out lie. Furthermore, he didn't think he was capable of sitting through three movies in a row.

However, he certainly wasn't going to allow her to walk out of his apartment alone when she was in a depressed state. "You mind if I go with you?"

She gave him a doubtful smile, as though she knew what a liar he was. But then she said, "I don't mind."

"You sure? I mean, if you have other plans—"

She chuckled. "You mean things I was going to do after I jumped off your ledge?"

"Something like that."

"No. That's about as far as I planned ahead."

Just what he liked: a woman who enjoyed black humor.

Chapter Four

"You met a woman who was in the process of attempting suicide and you took her to the movies?" Philly lifted off his baseball cap, smoothed back his hair, then returned the cap to its place atop his head. It was just one of his nervous mannerisms. Another was the three lit cigarettes in the ashtray on the bar.

"It's not as weird as it sounds," said Harry, squinting to see Philly through the smoke.

"It couldn't be. Nothing could possibly be as weird as that sounds, Harry."

"It's not as though she actually jumped."

"That's a relief. If I heard you'd taken a corpse to the movies I'd have you committed."

Harry debated telling him the next part, then thought, What the hell? If he couldn't tell it to an astro-shrink, who could he tell it to? "We saw three Bruce Lee movies. I haven't sat through three movies in a row since I was a kid."

"Did you sit in the balcony and make out?"

"Give me a break, Philly."

"Through three movies?"

Harry shook his head. "Come on, Philly, you don't try to make out with someone who's suicidal."

"No, of course not," agreed Philly. "What you do with someone who's suicidal is sit through three Bruce Lee movies. I tell you, Harry—I'd be suicidal if I had to sit through three of those."

"They cheered her up. You should've heard her, Philly. She was yelling and screaming, she and all those scary-looking guys who go to those movies."

Philly lit another cigarette. "Well, you did your duty, Harry. Now you can forget about her."

"I'd like to see her again."

Philly reached over and whisked off Harry's glasses. Then he peered into his friend's eyes.

"What're you doing?" asked Harry.

"I'm trying to determine whether you're on something."

"The only thing I'm on is three Budweisers, the same as you."

"She's a loser, my friend."

"Everyone's got problems."

"Just listen to me, Harry, okay? If I told you I had a woman I wanted you to meet, and then I told you she just lost her job and she was currently suicidal and the only way to cheer her up was to take her to Bruce Lee movies, would you be interested? And don't say yes or I'll call you a liar. You'd laugh in my face, Harry, that's what you'd do."

"At least she's different."

"Mental cases usually are different; that's what makes them mental cases."

"You're just used to thinking like a shrink."

"This isn't shrink talk, Harry; this is your buddy talking to you."

"I've got this problem."

"I can see that."

"Come on, Philly, don't I listen to you when you have problems?"

"I was just agreeing that you have a problem."

"All I know about her is her first name. No last name, no phone number, no address. And I know you're going to laugh, but I've got this idea that if we could just get to know each other, we'd be good together."

"So, you hang out at Bruce Lee movies."

"You mean there's more of them?"

"Or you scout available ledges around the city."

"There's got to be an easier way," said Harry.

"So, what do you think, Harry? Are the Mets going to make it to the playoffs?"

"I think they've got a better chance than I have of finding her again."

"IT'S NOT MY FAULT," said Jas, deciding to make a defiant last stand.

Pictures of a puppy frisking around a backyard, frisking around a living room and frisking around a bowl of Puppy Chow were spread across Stanley's desk.

Stanley's expression as he viewed the pictures left Jas in no doubt that he didn't find the puppy adorable. When he looked up at Jas it was obvious that he found her even less adorable than the puppy. "Didn't it occur to you to look at the photos before you left the drugstore?"

"No, it didn't, Stanley. The envelope had my name on it and the store was getting ready to close."

"And when did you look at them?"

"I was pretty surprised, Stanley, as you can imagine. I was also upset. I didn't sleep very well last night."

"And first thing this morning?" Stanley prompted her.

"I told you. I went back to the drugstore and insisted that the clerk go through every envelope of film that had been developed. There were no pictures of Mr. Capetto."

"So now someone, somewhere in this city, is the proud possessor of pictures of Mr. Capetto out of his wheelchair, while Paragon Investigations has nothing to hand over to the insurance company as evidence besides some badly taken pictures of a demented-looking puppy."

"Stanley, the clerk says that it's happened before and people always return the wrong pictures. Whoever took them probably wants those puppy pictures."

"Would you be willing to bet your job on that assumption?"

Jas subsided into silence.

Stanley pressed his fingertips to his temples and began a slow massage. "This isn't the first time something like this has happened to you, Jas."

"Yes, it is, Stanley. I've never gotten the wrong pictures before."

"If you would just develop your own film like the other investigators do—"

"You've never seen my bathroom. It doesn't even have room for a hair dryer, which is why my hair often looks wet when I get to work—"

"We're not discussing your hair, Jas."

"At least I had film in the camera this time."

"I'm glad you reminded me of that; I had forgotten that little episode. I was thinking of the Borchars case, which disappeared somewhere in your computer."

"It's only the technical stuff I ever have a problem with."

"It's become a technical business, Jas. And if you can't keep up with modern technology..." Stanley let the words trail off with a long-suffering sigh.

"I'm a master at disguise," said Jas, very much afraid that Stanley was about to fire her. He'd done it before, but on those occasions she had been able to talk him out of it.

"Jas, let me clue you in on something. We allow you your disguises because it makes you happy. But where in the investigator's manual is it written that being able to disguise yourself is a prerequisite for the job?"

"In the Fulton case—"

"The Fulton case? You really want to bring up the Fulton case, Jas?"

"My disguise was essential in that case."

"And why was it essential?"

"So that Mrs. Fulton wouldn't recognize me."

"But think, Jas. Why was there danger of your being recognized by Mrs. Fulton?"

Jas remembered too late. "I don't remember," she lied.

"Because you had mistaken Mrs. Fulton for her sister and made friends with her. Do you recall now?"

"Stanley, if you give me a chance, I know I can get Capetto again. And this time I swear I'll get Charlie to develop the film for me."

Stanley tilted his chair back and closed his eyes. Stanley's closing his eyes was usually an indication that Stanley was displeased. Since he already was displeased, however, she was afraid it boded worse.

Jas waited it out while Stanley appeared to take a nap. She felt really terrible about the whole thing, but at least she wouldn't be the hotshot detective anymore and maybe he'd take her off the Kingsley case. It went against her principles to go after someone who enjoyed Bruce Lee movies as much as she did.

When Stanley finally opened his eyes she thought she was going to be given a lecture. Instead, he looked surprised to see her. "What the hell are you doing in the office?" he asked her.

"I, uh, thought you were going to—"

"You're wasting time, Jas. Reopen the Capetto stakeout, and I mean right now. We've only got one more week before they go to court on this, and if you don't come up with something, a certain female investigator I know is going to be looking for another job. And without any references."

"Thank you for the vote of confidence, Stanley. I swear I won't let you down."

Stanley looked less than convinced.

JAS HAD JUST MADE Arnie one of her specials. It was a sandwich consisting of three slices of bologna, four slices of salami, a chunk of sharp cheddar, a slice of tomato, assorted cucumber slices and chunky peanut butter on an onion roll. She was trying to soften him up.

"I'd like to help you out, Jas," said Arnie, "but that's pretty unethical."

"It would be an accident," said Jas.

Arnie shook his head. "No, it wouldn't be an accident. It would be planned to look like an accident."

"It's not like he's really paralyzed."

"I don't care. I'm not going to run my bike into a man in a wheelchair and knock him over. He could sue my messenger service."

Jas couldn't help laughing. "Yeah, he probably could. But since he's already claiming he's paralyzed, I don't know what he could say you did to him."

"I have no intention of finding out."

"Arnie, I'm going to be fired if I don't get the pictures."

"I have every confidence in you."

"I'd have a lot more confidence if you'd run him down for me."

"Give it up, kid. I'm not going to do it. So, have you heard from that cartoonist?"

"His name's Harry, and I don't think he's called a cartoonist."

"Whatever. Have you heard from him?"

Jas reached across the table and grabbed the sandwich back from Arnie. "He doesn't have my phone number."

"So give him a call."

"What's the point, Arnie? He thinks I'm an unemployed computer programmer with suicidal ten-

dencies. Would you want to hear from someone like
that?"

"You really screwed it up, didn't you?"

"I did not. In fact, I was brilliant. Screwing it up
would have been either falling off the ledge or having
him find out I had broken into his apartment."

"I meant you screwed it up as far as a relationship
goes."

"Oh, well, I always screw those up."

THAT WEEK GROGAN took time out from his feud with
Kingsley's Department Store. Instead, Grogan, while
sunning himself on his fire escape, caught sight of a
pert Siamese cat hanging over the ledge of the building and contemplating suicide.

Two things happened. The first was that Grogan
became somewhat enamored of the sleek, elegant cat,
and second, Grogan, in pretty funny pseudopsychol-
ogy jargon, tried to talk the cat down.

On the third day of the strip, when the Siamese was
successfully persuaded to leap onto Grogan's fire escape, Jas finished reading the strip, ordered another
cup of coffee and headed for the phone booth in the
back of the coffee shop. It was the first time she could
ever remember that she hadn't been amused by Grogan's exploits.

She got Harry's number from information and
punched in the digits. She recognized his voice as soon
as he said hello.

"This is Jas."

"I was hoping you'd call. So, how are you? Things
going okay?"

"It's a little weird seeing myself in a comic strip."

"I didn't know how else to reach you. I don't even know your last name."

"My phone's unlisted, anyway." It was just one more lie to add to the already long list of lies she had told him. It wasn't unlisted at all; it was listed in the name of her deceased aunt.

"Are you at home?"

"Actually, I'm in a coffee shop on the Lower East Side. I was going to have breakfast."

"How about if I join you? I'd really like to see you."

"I don't think so."

"Why not? You're free at the moment, aren't you? I've been worried about you."

"I'm here for breakfast, Harry, not suicide. There's no reason to worry."

"Please. Just breakfast, okay? If you say yes, I'll drop it with the Siamese cat."

"That sounds like blackmail."

"Everything I say these days comes out sounding like blackmail."

Jas looked at her watch. Mr. Capetto wasn't due for his walk for another hour. "Okay, but only if you can get down here fast. I'm starved."

"I'm already hailing a cab," said Harry. "All I need is the address."

Jas was pretty sure she was making a mistake.

HARRY WALKED into the coffee shop, looked around and saw nothing but punkers, and was turning around to leave when he heard her calling him.

He turned back, still didn't see her and wondered if he needed stronger lenses. Then he noticed one of the punkers waving at him.

He walked toward the table and the closer he got the more she looked vaguely familiar, but she still didn't look like Jas. Then when he saw it actually was Jas, albeit an exceedingly weird-looking Jas, he joined her at her table. He couldn't help wondering why a yuppie would overnight turn into a punker.

She looked nervous. She smiled at him; then her eyes went to the window. He had never been attracted to women who wore their hair in stiff spikes and whose makeup made them resemble vampires. And yet he had noticed that the women who aspired to that look usually had thin, pointy faces and androgynous bodies. Jas's face was softly rounded and her body, while small and slender, was far from androgynous.

"It's good to see you again," said Harry.

Her eyes flickered briefly in his direction before returning to the window. "I already ordered. I hope you don't mind."

"Sorry, the traffic was horrendous." Judging by the remains on her plate she hadn't enjoyed her meal. "What would you recommend?"

"Nothing, really. They don't have very good food."

"You live around here?"

"No."

Which meant she was the kind of person who would travel to get to a bad restaurant. That should tell him something about her, but just what he wasn't certain. He was beginning to wonder why he had wanted to see her. She had seemed animated at the movies, but now she appeared to be merely watchful.

Harry called the waiter over and ordered eggs. The very worst of restaurants usually didn't ruin eggs. "Would you like some more coffee?" he asked her.

"No. Six cups is about my limit."

Six cups? He could think of no reason to sit in a bad restaurant and drink six cups of coffee unless she were steeling herself to do something. Perhaps she had been steeling herself to call him. If so, he found it rather touching.

"I would've asked you for your phone number," he said, "but you seemed to disappear into thin air when we got out of the movies."

"I wasn't myself that day."

He hoped she meant the suicidal thoughts and not the mode of dress. If he had seen a punker on his ledge he wasn't sure if he would've wanted to talk her down. In fact, he might have joined the chorus that had been urging her to jump. Not that he had any great love for the yuppies, but at least they didn't resemble another species entirely.

"What is your phone number? Unless, of course, you'd rather not hear from me."

"I wouldn't mind hearing from you."

Harry took a pen out of his pocket and one of his cards and shoved them across the table. "Perhaps you'd write down your number for me."

She wrote down the numbers so slowly he was sure she was making up the number. But if she was giving him a phony number, why call him up to begin with? As he was pocketing the card, he wondered what Grogan would think of a punk cat. He had a good idea that a punk cat wouldn't at all appeal to Grogan, and yet there was still something about Jas that appealed to him. If nothing else, the mystery of the reason behind her transformation. He couldn't wait to hear what Philly would say about this recent development.

"Any luck getting a job?" he inquired, hoping to get a conversation started.

"No."

"Did you take my advice and form a tenants' association?"

"Not yet."

Harry, who had had better conversations with strangers on the subway, gave up, sat back and waited for his eggs to arrive.

She didn't appear to find the silence disturbing. Her attention seemed to be riveted on the sidewalk outside the restaurant, where other punkers drifted by. Maybe she was patiently waiting to get back to her own people. Maybe she found him as odd as he was finding her.

Just when he thought she had forgotten him completely, she said, "Have you finished with Kingsley?"

"You mean Grogan?"

She gave a slight nod.

"Oh, no, Grogan's just getting started."

"Oh, I thought since you were doing something different, the thing with Kingsley was over." He could swear she didn't look happy at the news.

"I've never used the strip for anything like that before, but I couldn't think of any other way to get in touch with you. Maybe I could've put a personal ad in, but I didn't know whether you read those, and I knew you read Grogan."

"Why'd you make me a Siamese?" She hated Siamese cats. Her grandmother had had one and it was always whining.

"There's something elegant and exotic about them. I just thought it would be an intriguing sort of cat for Grogan to spot on his ledge."

"Kind of the yuppie of cats?" asked Jas.

Harry shook his head. "Cats are too independent to be part of a group."

His breakfast arrived, which momentarily diverted his attention away from her. He was buttering his cold toast and was about to ask her if she had changed her opinion of Kingsley's when she shot out of her chair, reached into her bag and slammed some money down on the table, then said, "Sorry, Harry, I have to go," and was racing for the door before he could stop her.

He took a good look at his eggs and decided he could live without them. In fact, he'd probably live a lot longer without them. He left Jas's money for a tip, then went up to the cash register and paid for his breakfast.

"Something wrong with your eggs?" asked the cashier, who was dressed almost exactly like Jas.

"Not really," said Harry.

The guy was nodding. "Bad karma. I understand."

Harry didn't understand at all but was glad he was getting out of there without being made to feel guilty about not eating his eggs. His mother wouldn't have let him off so easily.

When he got out on the sidewalk and saw Jas in the next block, leisurely strolling along, he wondered why she had been in such a hurry to leave. So he hadn't been such great company. She hadn't exactly been scintillating herself. Not that she had been enthusiastic about his offer to join her for breakfast. If he were honest with himself, he'd have to admit that the only logical reason for her agreeing to it was that she was afraid he was going to expose her in the comic strip. He wouldn't have done something like that. He wouldn't have humiliated her in public, naming her and telling everyone she had considered killing herself. She must think he was a pretty rotten person if she were afraid of something like that.

He saw her duck into a store up ahead, but seconds later she was back on the sidewalk again walking slowly as though she had nothing else to do. Since he had nothing else to do, he figured he'd follow her for a while. Maybe she'd get in a better mood by lunchtime and they could try again.

He noticed a man in a wheelchair being pushed across the street and then entering a small park. Harry had heard tales about that small park and it wasn't the kind of place he wanted to frequent, but soon he saw that Jas was also crossing over to the park. He hoped she wasn't headed for the park for the reason most people headed for that park. Although if she were, it might explain her erratic behavior.

Harry hadn't realized it was so easy to follow someone and remain undetected. Not once had she turned around, and she apparently had no idea Harry was close behind. He wondered if it were an invasion of her privacy to be following her. He decided that it wasn't nearly as much an invasion of her privacy as his latest comic strip had been. And how was he supposed to get to know her if he didn't invade her privacy?

She was following the path that cut through the park and only at one point did she do something unexpected. At the far end of the park he saw her step off the path and peer into some bushes for a moment. This seemed strange, but no stranger than other things about her. But he was soon to see something so bizarre that peering into the bushes became almost normal behavior.

It happened as he got to the end of the park and was once again stepping onto a sidewalk. He spotted the man in the wheelchair across the street, but the person who had been pushing him was nowhere in sight. Who was in sight was Jas, and she appeared to be creeping up behind the wheelchair.

That was patently ridiculous. Why would she be creeping up behind a wheelchair?

The reason was soon apparent. She had been creeping up behind the wheelchair in order to grab hold of it and start tilting it so precariously that the occupant was sure to fall out onto the sidewalk.

Harry couldn't believe what he was seeing. Perhaps she was capable of suicide, but he never would have expected her to be the kind of person who was capable of harming a handicapped person. And yet there she was, rocking the wheelchair with ever-greater intensity as the occupant was screaming for help and hanging on to the sides of the chair for dear life.

Just as Harry was deciding to go to the man's rescue even if it meant never seeing Jas again, she did such a dastardly thing that Harry was incapable of even breathing for a few seconds. She shoved the wheelchair in the direction of the street, where it was sure to end up in the path of an oncoming car.

As he started to rush forward to signal the car to stop, he saw the handicapped person jump out of the chair and furiously start in Jas's direction. Harry shifted his attention to Jas, who was calmly snapping a picture of the man. And then, as the man was about to attack her, his hand already reaching for the camera, Jas looked up and saw Harry across the street and yelled, "Catch, Harry," and threw the camera over the top of the car that was slowing down in order to avoid hitting the wheelchair. Harry reached up and made a beautiful one-handed catch.

"Run, Harry," yelled Jas, and he could see that the man's attention had been diverted by the throw just long enough for Jas to take off running west. She was damn fast and had disappeared around the corner before Harry could yell, "Why?"

Now Harry saw the man coming after him, and he took off back through the park, carrying the camera under his arm as though it were a football. He didn't stop running until he exited the park at the other end, and then, when he looked around and saw he was no longer being chased, he sauntered out of the park and wondered what to do next. He was now the proud possessor of a picture of a man jumping out of a wheelchair. He wondered what in the world he would do with it.

JAS RETURNED to the coffee shop in the hopes that Harry would meet her there. When he still hadn't shown up after thirty minutes, she started to worry that maybe Mr. Capetto had caught up with Harry and confiscated the camera. So it was with great relief that she saw Mr. Capetto being wheeled back to his apartment and there was no camera at all in sight. The expression on his face was priceless. He looked exactly like a little boy who had been deprived of his candy. A nasty little boy.

Jas decided to head over to her apartment and get out of her disguise. She didn't want to go back to the office until she had the film in her hand to present to Stanley, and she also didn't want to hear any of Charlie's remarks that he made every time she showed up looking punk. Also, this way she could go back on the bike and get in some lease-police business the rest of the day.

She had no sooner gotten the mousse out of her hair and the gunk off her face than the phone rang. She hoped it was Harry.

It was. "I have something of yours," he said.

"Great. I really appreciated your help."

"My pleasure," said Harry, sounding very much as though he were trying to be sarcastic. He wasn't succeeding.

"Where are you? I'll meet you and pick it up."

"Where are you?"

"I'm at home," said Jas.

"I'm aware of that. What I meant was where do you live?"

"You don't have to come all the way over here, Harry."

"I don't mind." He was sounding determined.

"Where are you now?"

"Sixth Avenue and Eighth Street."

"All right," said Jas, relenting. "You're pretty close. I guess you might as well come over."

As soon as she had given him directions, she raced out of the building and down the street to a building she knew was going co-op. With her burglar tools, she removed the sign from the lobby and within minutes had put it up in the foyer of her building. She didn't want Harry to catch her in any lies if she could help it.

When Harry arrived she ignored the look he directed at her hair. "Thanks," she said, practically snatching the camera out of his hand.

"Cozy place," he said, eyeing the living area, which would have fit into one corner of his living room. "I saw the sign downstairs. Every time I see one of those I get depressed."

She realized she didn't know how to get the film out of the camera, so instead she put the whole thing in her bag to give to Charlie. "Well, thanks again, Harry," she said, hoping he'd get the message and leave.

"I didn't get breakfast," he said. "How about joining me for lunch?"

"I've got peanut butter and salami if you'd like me to make you a sandwich."

Harry looked a little thrown. "I think I'll pass on that, Jas, but there are some good restaurants around here."

She forced herself to relax. After all, she got the pictures, Stanley would be appeased and she deserved a lunch hour, didn't she?

"Okay," she said, thinking she could come back after lunch and get into her messenger-service gear.

When they got downstairs three other tenants were in the lobby, all three of them bemoaning the fact that their building was going co-op. A concerned-looking Harry said, "What you people should do is form a tenants' association and fight it."

Jas hustled him out of there fast.

Harry didn't say a word until they were eating their hamburgers. Then, very casually, he said, "Was there some reason for taking that man's picture?"

Jas managed to smile with her mouth full. "I'm something of an amateur photographer." She hoped he didn't know any more about cameras than she did.

"I see. What exactly do you specialize in?"

"People. You know, New York characters. I find the street people pretty interesting."

"Do you always set up your pictures?"

Jas, who hadn't been sure how much Harry had seen, now began to think he had seen more than she thought. "Oh, you mean Johnny. That was just a joke. We're old friends; we're always fooling around like that."

Harry didn't look convinced. "Johnny didn't seem to have a sense of humor."

"That's just Johnny's way."

"From where I was standing, he looked pretty angry."

"He was putting it on."

"Well, he convinced me."

"He used to be an actor." Lying to Harry seemed to get easier with practice.

"If it's not too personal a question, just why is that friend of yours riding around in a wheelchair?"

"I told you, he has a sense of humor. It's kind of his personal backlash against people who jog. He really hates joggers." Jas made a point of looking at her watch. "I hate to eat and run, Harry, but I've got a job interview in a little while and I want to change my clothes."

She figured he'd give her an argument about it. Or offer to walk her home. Or at least tell her he'd call her later. He did none of the above. In fact, unless she was really mistaken, he looked greatly relieved when she left him there. What a shame it was that when she finally met a really nice guy, all events seemed to be conspiring to make sure nothing ever came of it.

When she got back to her building a furious Arnie ran down the steps to greet her. "You're not going to believe this, Jas. This is just too much, too much."

"Hi, Arnie," said Jas.

"Our building's going co-op."

"Oh, is that what's bothering you? I put that sign up. I guess I better take it back down."

"You mean it's not true?"

"Not yet."

"I'm sure you had a good reason."

"Harry was here. So I had to put a sign up because I had already told him our building was going co-op. That was the primary reason for the suicide attempt, you know."

"Of course. How could I have forgotten?"

"And, Arnie, I got Capetto!"

"Hey, congratulations. How did you manage that? Did you get Harry to run him down in a car?"

Jas gave him a smug look. "I didn't need his help; I did it all by myself. The nerve of that man trying to pretend he's paralyzed."

"Yeah," said Arnie. "Just think of that. Isn't it amazing what some people will do to fool others?"

"I see it every day in this business," said Jas.

"Like some people will actually fake a suicide attempt."

"It's not the same, Arnie. Capetto was doing it for money."

"You mean you'd have done it if Stanley hadn't been paying you, Jas?"

"Why are you giving me a hard time, Arnie?"

"Somebody has to. So what was Harry doing here?"

"He had the camera. I had to throw it to him when Capetto was going after me."

"Wait a minute, Jas—hold on. Are you saying that Harry Keyes was an accessory to this?"

"No. I was following Capetto and he was following me, that's all. I told him Capetto was a friend of mine."

"And he believed that?"

"He seems pretty gullible, Arnie. He believes everything I tell him."

"Poor man," said Arnie.

KING WAS HAVING a fantasy of a somewhat sexual nature.

Because he lived in his penthouse and never left it, his fantasies were limited to women he saw on television, or the occasional woman in a building across the street seen through his telescope, or, on rare occasions, an office temp his private secretary hired when the work load became too great for her to handle on her own.

Women seen on his television screen weren't satisfactory because they weren't real. This didn't mean he didn't like watching them; only that they weren't prime fantasy material. When he would zoom in on a woman in one of the other buildings on Fifth Avenue it was interesting, but it was also during working hours as none of the buildings contained apartments. And King didn't like wasting business hours on fantasies.

The occasional office temp might loosen his libido in a fantasy or two, but these were marred by the fact that they never provided any intellectual stimulation. He found he could easily imagine them typing, but it was much more difficult to imagine them ravishing his body.

The king was no monk. He felt that sex was almost as important to his health as enough food, and to fulfill this need Teddy would, once a week, arrange for a woman to visit King in his penthouse. On these occasions King would indulge in fantasy-free sex.

Now, however, King had someone who appeared to fill the bill as a perfect fantasy figure. Jas was adorable, she was bright, she was in an interesting line of work, and she appeared to be worthy of being a candidate of his fantasies.

Best of all, she didn't show him the proper respect, which was a real turn-on. Up until now he had found that being a billionaire drew respect from every woman he met.

Her eyes were the color of chocolate bonbons, her cheeks were as soft as whipped cream, her mouth was as pink and juicy as rare roast beef and her small teeth glistened like frosting. He fantasized seducing her over a twelve-course meal.

She was absolutely delectable.

Chapter Five

Floyd "The King" Kingsley was sitting in on the latest presentation by his ad agency. Because the King equated obscurity with failure, he made it a point to have every aspect of both his personal life and his business life publicized. To this end he had a press agent, a publicity department and the services of the best ad agency in the city. The King was dedicated to the notion that the only day his name might conceivably not appear in the papers would be the day after his obituary ran.

The latest advertising campaign was to be in three parts: newspapers, one-minute TV spots and billboards. It went like this: "You don't have to be a fat cat to shop at Kingsley's. In fact, it helps if you aren't."

The King watched the presentation in silence. At the end of it, when his minions were waiting to either smile or frown, depending on his reaction, King sat in silence for a while. It wasn't that he was ambivalent; it was more that he truly enjoyed seeing people squirm.

He finally posed a **que**stion of the account executive. "You're not actually going to use cats, are you?" The King abhorred cats.

"No, no," the account executive assured him. "Fat cat in this sense means people with money."

"I have money," said King.

"What it actually means," said the account executive, who was now beginning to lose his composure, "is that you don't have to be rich to shop at Kingsley's, and—and this part is a little dig at the comic-strip cat—it might even help if you're not Grogan."

King, who had known all along what it meant and had merely wanted to prolong everyone's discomfort, sat back and crossed his arms over his considerable stomach. "I think I...like it," he said, and waited for the smiles of relief to appear. "In fact, I know I like it. But I think you could use one cat and use it judiciously." When he had finished explaining to them what he wanted, there were sneaky smiles all around.

The King said, "I want it out there immediately. And if not immediately, at least by tomorrow."

As the ad-agency people filed out of his office, King said, "Teddy, I want to see you for a minute."

When they were alone, King said, "What's happening with that detective?" He was dying to see her again in the flesh.

"I don't know, sir."

"Well, get on the phone and find out. Better yet, tell her I want to see her in my office with a full report." Seeing her again would satisfy two of his current fantasies: the one dealing with Jas and the one dealing with Harry.

The King loved revenge but didn't love having to wait for it. He wanted to see Harry Keyes squeezed until he squirmed. And then, while he was still squirming, he wanted him completely demolished.

Totalitarianism was alive and well in Kingsley Tower.

"YOU'VE REDEEMED YOURSELF," said Stanley. "The pictures came out clear as a bell. You would have saved the agency both time and money, however, if you had done it right the first time."

Jas was trying not to stare at Stanley's hair. She could only surmise he had been caught in the noon downpour as the hair, which was formally bouffant, was now bedraggled and hanging every which way across the top of Stanley's head. She would purposely avert her eyes and stare out the window, only to have them drawn back again and again. She had an urge to recommend her brand of mousse to him. He was undoubtedly using hair spray, which didn't hold up nearly as well. She managed to quell the urge in the interests of keeping her job.

"How did you manage to get him out of the wheelchair a second time? I would think, with the court date approaching, he would have been more cautious."

"You really don't want to hear, Stanley."

Stanley looked as though he might give her an argument about that, but then he changed tack. "Kingsley wants to see you in his office first thing tomorrow morning."

"I wish you'd send someone else. I'd like to be taken off that if it's possible."

"Do you have any idea how much money he's paying us?"

"Not us," said Jas. "The agency."

"If you get him what he wants, there could be a bonus in it for you."

"Stanley, we're talking about a nice decent man, and I'm not referring to Kingsley. First of all, he's a legal tenant."

Stanley waited for a moment, then said, "And second of all?"

"There's a conflict of interest here."

"Please be more precise."

"I sort of became friends with him."

Stanley shot forward in his chair so fast that strands of his hair seemed to float momentarily in the air. "You did what?"

"I got to know him a little. I like him."

"Appearances to the contrary, Jas, we are not running a dating service here. What we're running is an investigative agency. How, might I ask, did you get to know him?"

"I don't think you want to know that, either."

"Jas, one of the first things you should've learned is that if you're going to have qualms, you're in the wrong profession. If we got a job to investigate your mother, then I'd expect you to investigate her."

She knew that wasn't entirely Stanley's avarice speaking; they had taught her the same thing in detective school. "Kingsley wants me to get something on him. I don't think there's anything to get. What if he's clean, Stanley?"

"Nobody's clean."

"Well, I don't think I'm going to be able to find anything."

"And you call yourself an investigator? Do you remember the first day you walked in here, Jas? Do you remember what you said to me?"

"Not exactly."

"Well, I remember exactly. What you said was it was your lifelong ambition to be a private investigator. You said that if I gave you a chance, you'd never let me down. Do you recall that, Jas?"

She recalled being desperate after every other agency in the yellow pages had turned her down. "I guess so."

"Have you decided to change professions?"

"No. I love the work. Usually. I'd just prefer not having this case."

"Request denied, Jas."

That was Stanley at his understanding best.

"WAIT A MINUTE," said Philly. "Let me get this straight. She tried to shove some old guy in a wheelchair into the path of a car?"

Harry was nervously shuffling the cards. "That's about it, Philly."

"And she was dressed like a punker?"

Harry nodded, his hands moving faster and faster.

"And then she gave you some song and dance about being an amateur photographer?"

The cards sprayed out of his hands and all over the room.

"Pick up the tarot cards, Harry, and pull yourself together. You want a beer?"

"I could use one."

Philly reached over to the pint-sized refrigerator he kept in his office and got them each a Bud. "Do you happen to know her sign?"

"What's her sign got to do with anything?"

Philly pulled down the peak of his Mets cap and gave Harry a moment to collect himself and to have a little beer. "My friend, either you've gotten yourself mixed up with an insane homicidal maniac with a split personality besides being potentially suicidal, or there's more here than meets the eye. I just thought if she were a Gemini it might explain why she's a yuppie one day and a punker the next."

"The dumb part of it is, I think you'd like her, Philly."

"I'd like her as a client. If I could do her chart, maybe I could find out what went wrong with her."

Harry picked up the crystal ball out of its stand and began to toss it up and down. "What'd you mean when you said there was more here than meets the eye?"

"If you drop that, Harry, you owe me forty bucks."

"I'm not going to drop it. You should've seen the catch I made when she threw me the camera. You would've been proud of me."

"To answer your question, even the most mixed-up of my clients don't come off as bizarre as this new interest of yours."

"So?"

"So maybe there's a reason for all this strange behavior. And maybe if we found that reason, it would all make sense."

"You really believe that, Philly? That there could be some logical reason?"

"It's rather stretching credulity."

"I'd like you to meet her."

"Give her my card."

"No, Philly, not like that. You don't tell some woman you want to see that she ought to go to a shrink."

"An astro-shrink."

"That, either. What I was thinking was I could ask her to meet me for a drink. And you could be there."

"That should be interesting."

"You don't have to tell her what you do. Just act like a regular person, you know?"

"I'll try," Philly started to say, but his attention was diverted by the trajectory his crystal ball was taking. A moment later he said, "That's forty bucks you owe me, Harry. Plus the cost of having the window replaced."

A COLD FRONT was supposed to move in the next day. Since it might be the last balmy evening before autumn set in, Jas and Arnie were sitting outside at one of the neighborhood sidewalk cafés enjoying espressos.

"I could get you a job as a messenger," Arnie was saying. "You're real fast on that bike; you'd be great at it. And I bring home more than you do every week. Plus, it's honest work, Jas."

"You make it sound like I'm a criminal."

"Well, I mean, throwing some guy out of a wheelchair?"

"He was trying to cheat an insurance company out of millions. So, my approach was a little unorthodox. I was up against the wall."

"What if he hadn't jumped out of the chair? What if he'd been run over?"

"That was his decision. But if he was capable of jumping out and he didn't, I'd call it suicide."

"The police wouldn't have called it suicide. For all intents and purposes, he was paralyzed. It would've been your word against everyone else's."

"Well, I'm not interested in being a messenger. I mean, I'm finding it fun, but that's only because I'm really something else. It's kind of a dead-end job, Arnie."

"That's where you're wrong. Someday I'll open my own messenger service."

"And someday I'll open my own agency. You've got to understand, Arnie, I've wanted to be a detective since I was nine years old and read the Freddie books."

"Come again?"

"They were about a pig named Freddie who was a detective."

"I never read those."

"Well, they were wonderful. They shaped my life."

"I used to like Batman."

"See? And now you're a messenger."

"I don't see the connection, Jas."

"Well, you fly around on your bike, don't you?"

"All right, but you wouldn't be having this problem with Harry now if you weren't a private investigator."

"I wouldn't have met him if I weren't a private investigator."

"You really like him, huh?"

Jas nodded.

"The problem is, Jas, if he likes you, he's got to have a screw loose."

"Thanks a lot, Arnie."

"Use your head. Would you like a potential suicide who pushes people in wheelchairs in front of cars?"

"I have wondered about that. In fact, I wondered why he didn't walk out of the coffee shop when he saw me in that punker getup."

"You look pretty cute in that."

"But strange. And he's not strange at all. He's a regular person. And nice."

"And straight. And single."

Jas nodded. "There aren't many of those around."

"You want my advice, Jas? You want some really sensible advice?"

"That's what I'm hoping for."

"Cool it until you've finished the investigation. Then you can explain to him why you acted the way you did."

"You don't think he'd mind when I told him I was investigating him for Kingsley?"

"It's not like it's personal. It's your job."

"You think he'd be that understanding?"

"Listen, if he didn't freak over the wheelchair, I don't think he'd freak over that."

"I'll think about it. Do you want to go back to my place and watch the Mets game?"

"Okay by me. I've had about all the espresso I can take for one night."

SHE DID THINK about it. She thought about it all the way home, but there was one problem. By the time the investigation was over, Harry would've forgotten about her. In fact, he looked as though he'd just about forgotten about her when she left him after lunch.

But Arnie was right. How could she possibly like someone who liked someone like her, or the way she appeared to be whenever he saw her? She might have gone out with some less-than-perfect men, but none of them had tried to jump off her building or kill someone in a wheelchair. If they had, she would've run in the other direction fast. The guy had some real problems if he was attracted to her.

And since she couldn't see any problems attached to Harry Keyes, she had to suppose he wasn't attracted. After all, she had called him today; he hadn't called her. And if he had wanted to see her, she was sure it was just the Good Samaritan coming out in him, the concern that anyone might have for someone who only days before had been suicidal. He was just a good citizen, that's all; a good human being. Not to mention sexy, although that had nothing to do with anything at the moment.

And one of the tenets of being a good private investigator was not getting mixed up with people like that. Because if you did, then maybe the next thing that would happen would be you'd suddenly develop a guilty conscience about your work—and that spelled disaster.

They were watching the game, Arnie sprawled across her bed and Jas on the floor, when the phone rang. Jas reached for it and said hello, her eyes on a double play. Then, for a moment, it felt as though the game were in stereo as she was hearing it over the phone as well as in the room.

"Jas? What're you doing?"

"Who is this?" asked Jas. She could barely hear over the noise of the game.

"Harry."

Jas glanced over at Arnie and caught his eye. "Oh, hi, Harry." Arnie started shaking his head as though warning her not to talk to him.

"How about coming out for a drink?"

Jas contemplated getting up off the floor and actually going out. It seemed like too much trouble. "I don't know, Harry. It's kind of late. But I appreciate your asking."

"Late? This is New York. The bars stay open until four, in case you didn't know it."

"Yeah, but—"

"It's not as though you have to get up and go to work in the morning. Hey, how did your job interview go?"

"My job interview? Oh, yeah, that. It went fine. I mean, I didn't get the job, but it was okay."

"Come on. You can watch the baseball game with me."

"I'm watching it here."

"Hey, Jas, you want to hear this great idea I have? For Grogan?"

She relaxed a little. "Sure, let's hear it."

"Well, you've got to be able to visualize this. Here's Grogan, walking through the park, minding his own business. You seeing it?"

"Yeah, I'm seeing it."

"And then he sees something he can't quite believe. There's the Siamese cat he had met on his fire escape and the Siamese cat is shoving this guy in a wheelchair into the path—"

"Are you trying to blackmail me again, Harry?" she shouted into the phone.

"I'm only trying to get you to come out for a drink. Listen, we're not far from you. I'm having a few beers with my friend Philly."

"Hold on a minute, Harry." She put her hand over the receiver and said to Arnie, "Want to go meet him for a drink?"

"He's blackmailing you?"

"Yeah, with Grogan again. So what do you say? Want to meet him?"

"I doubt whether I was invited."

"He's got a friend with him, I don't see why I can't have a friend with me."

Arnie nodded. "Yeah, I'd like to meet him."

Jas spoke into the receiver. "Okay, Harry, you're on. Tell me where you are and we'll meet you there."

"We?"

"I'm with a friend, too. Is that okay?"

"Couldn't be better," said Harry, who was no doubt picturing fixing his friend up with her friend. Harry was in for a surprise.

HARRY WAS SURPRISED, all right. He had just gotten through warning Philly, "Be prepared for anything," when into the bar walked a perfectly normal-looking woman wearing perfectly normal-looking clothes; in fact, the same kind of clothes he and Philly were wearing. She had a nice smile on her face, not at all the smile a suicide or a murderer would have. And with her was a perfectly normal-looking guy.

Harry wasn't thrilled about that last part.

"That's her," he said, diverting Philly's attention from the game.

"Where?"

"The one in the jeans and sweater."

Philly did a double take. "She doesn't look weird to me."

Harry waved to Jas, gesturing for her to come to his end of the bar. "Just give her five minutes and I'll bet she does something bizarre."

"I can't wait," said Philly.

Harry was bringing an empty bar stool and putting it between his and Philly's when Jas and her friend got down to them. "I'd like you to meet my friend, Philly," he said.

"I'd like you to meet my friend, Arnie," she countered.

Luckily, what might have been an awkward moment was helped by a Mets home run, and by the time the hitter had rounded home plate, Jas was on the bar stool, Arnie and Philly were shaking hands, and Harry was ordering them all beer.

"Jas and I are neighbors," Arnie said to him, which clarified the situation enough so that Harry was able to smile at him benignly.

"Sorry to hear about your building," said Harry.

Arnie looked confused. "My building?"

"Yeah, going co-op. It's happening to mine and I know what you're going through."

"What's your sign?" Philly was asking Jas.

"I love your comic strip," Arnie said to Harry.

"Thanks," said Harry, as Jas was saying, "I don't believe in that stuff."

"I'm an Aries," said Arnie, but Philly didn't seem interested.

Jas said, "I didn't know you were into astrology, Arnie."

"I read my horoscope every day. Don't you?"

Philly said to Jas, "I have a feeling you're a Gemini."

"What you need is a tenants' association," said Harry.

Philly said, "Now, my friend Harry here is a Libra, which right away tells you he's pretty easygoing."

"Not always," said Harry, not wanting Jas to think he was some wishy-washy Pisces. Not that he believed in it.

"I'd say Grogan is pretty easygoing," said Arnie.

"Don't tell me," Jas said to Philly. "You're the astro-shrink."

"What's an astro-shrink?" asked Arnie.

Philly said, "Did Harry tell you about me?"

Harry was trying very hard to fade into the woodwork.

"He didn't exactly tell me about you," Jas said, "but when I was standing on his ledge he asked if I'd like him to call an astro-shrink."

"You didn't tell me that part," said Arnie.

"Did you hear the one about the shaggy dog?" Harry asked, but everyone ignored him. He was trying very hard to remember why it had seemed like a good idea for Philly to meet Jas.

Philly said to Jas, "I'd really like to do your chart. Free of charge, of course."

"I wouldn't mind having mine done," said Arnie.

"Listen, guys, why don't we watch the ball game?" said Jas.

"You a Mets fan?" Harry asked her.

"Of course I'm a Mets fan. I grew up in Queens."

"So did I," said Harry. "Philly and I both."

"I grew up in New Jersey," said Arnie.

Philly said, "If you're not a Gemini, then I bet you're a Leo. Except the hair's not right. Leos usually have big manes of hair."

"I wouldn't mind a big mane of hair," said Arnie, whose hairline was receding.

"It doesn't matter what I am because I don't believe in it," said Jas.

"I agree," said Harry.

"It's kind of like poverty," Philly explained. "You might not believe in it, but it's still there."

Three confused faces looked in his direction.

"Well, maybe that was a bad analogy."

"So, what do you do for a living?" Harry asked Arnie. Not that he was particularly interested, but it had to be more interesting than astrology.

"I'm a messenger," said Arnie.

"Yeah? Maybe I've seen you. I get stuff by messenger all the time."

Arnie seemed about to open his mouth to say something when Harry saw Jas shove her elbow in his side. Arnie's mouth didn't open and Harry was left wondering what that was all about.

"Maybe Capricorn," said Philly, who never knew when a subject was dead. "Capricorns don't like to talk about themselves."

Jas folded her arms across her chest. "If I could be a Gemini or a Leo or a Capricorn equally well, then obviously there's no method to it."

Philly gave her a sheepish smile. "You're right. I'll stick with my first guess. Only a Gemini could act the way you act."

"The way I act?"

"How do Geminis act?" asked Arnie.

"Some of them have split personalities."

"Why do you think I have a split personality?" asked Jas. "You don't even know me."

Harry thought it was now his turn to shove an elbow in Philly's side but he wasn't close enough to do it.

Philly, who seemed to be sensing he had walked into a trap, merely shrugged.

"Let me guess," said Jas. "Because I was on Harry's ledge acting suicidal the other day and tonight I'm drinking a beer and watching a ball game, that gives me a split personality, right? What does that mean, that I should be consistent and attempt suicide every day?"

"She's really not the suicidal type," said Arnie.

"You're absolutely right," said Philly. "I've been jumping to conclusions. In fact, I'd hazard a guess that you're an easygoing Libra like Harry."

"I'm definitely not a Libra," said Jas, and Harry wondered what she meant by that.

"I like you; you're okay," said Philly, and in a gesture of goodwill, took off his baseball cap and put it on Jas's head.

And Harry instantly recognized her as the messenger. The phony messenger, as it had turned out when he'd tried to find the Aim-to-Please Messenger Service in the phone book. Split personality? Oh, no, she didn't have a split personality. She had a multiple personality. He wondered what sign that would be.

Jas finished off her beer, handed Philly's baseball cap back to him and said, "Thanks for the beer, Harry. It was a pleasure meeting you, Philly, but I think Arnie and I are going to call it an evening. Say good-night, Arnie."

Arnie said good-night and they both left before Harry could think of any reason to keep them there. He wasn't even sure he wanted to keep them there, not when he was dying to tell Philly the latest development.

"She's okay," said Philly. "She didn't seem strange at all. Yeah, I liked her. You've got my approval, Harry."

"Not so fast," said Harry. "She was the messenger."

"What messenger?"

"I didn't tell you that part," said Harry. "But then, I hadn't known it was connected." He told Philly about Jas's posing as a messenger.

"She seemed so normal," said Philly.

"Can you make any sense out of it?"

"It sounds like the kind of ploy a groupie would use to meet a rock star."

"I'm not a rock star," Harry reminded him.

"Yeah, but there are other kinds of groupies. Consider this scenario, Harry. Here's one of your fans, loves Grogan, is dying to meet the talented creator of that popular comic strip. So she dresses up as a messenger and shows up at your door."

"And then comes back and tries to jump off my ledge?"

"Why not? She meets you at your door, falls madly in love with you and then shows up on your ledge, knowing she'll get your sympathy."

"As a yuppie?"

"Well, you didn't fall for the messenger, so maybe she figured you liked yuppies. After all, you do live on the Upper West Side."

"Oh, yeah, right. So, then, just to keep all her options open, the next time she sees me she dresses up like a punker and tries to kill some old man, just to get me really interested."

"You're missing the point, Harry. It might sound bizarre, but she did succeed. You are getting rather obsessed with her."

"Couldn't she have just written me a fan letter?"

"She's obviously more creative than that."

"I find it a little hard to believe that anyone would want to meet me badly enough to go through all that."

"You should feel flattered."

"What if I hadn't been home that day? Would she have jumped just to get my attention?"

"Speaking as a shrink, Harry, she didn't seem suicidal to me."

"She wasn't suicidal tonight. Although she might have become suicidal if you had kept up that astrological stuff much longer."

"So. Do you like my theory?"

"No. It might make sense, but I don't like it. It makes me feel stalked. I like to be the one to do the stalking."

"You might think you like to, but you're too easy-going. You usually give up too easily."

"Well, she's interesting; you've got to admit that."

"Never a dull moment. I wonder what she'll be next?"

"WHY'D WE LEAVE SO SOON?" asked Arnie as they were walking home.

"Didn't you see what he was up to? He had told that astro-shrink all about me, and the guy was trying to analyze me."

"Do you blame him?"

"I don't blame Philly; I blame Harry. He has a lot of nerve telling all those personal things about me to his friend."

"You told me."

"That's different."

"Be realistic, Jas. The poor guy is probably trying to figure you out. I would be if I were in his shoes."

"Gemini! What a lot of nonsense."

"What sign are you, Jas?"

"I don't believe in that!"

"I'd still like to know."

"I'm a Gemini," said Jas, and they both burst out laughing. "And it doesn't mean a split personality; it means I like to live a double life. Which is true. Which is why being a private investigator is perfect for me."

"Just one thing," said Arnie. "He doesn't look like John Denver."

"Sure he does. He has sandy-colored hair, blue eyes and wears glasses."

"But he doesn't look like John Denver. He's taller, he's got a thinner face, his nose is different—"

"It was easier saying he looked like John Denver than trying to describe him. Anyway, at the time I never thought you'd meet him."

"Yes, but I would've spent the rest of my life picturing Grogan's creator as looking like John Denver."

"Sorry, Arnie."

"That's okay. I don't like John Denver anyway. So why'd you drag me out of there so fast? I was enjoying those guys."

"I was uncomfortable."

"In a bar? Since when are you uncomfortable in a bar?" asked Arnie.

"It's not being in a bar; it's being around Harry. It makes me uncomfortable being around him when I'm attracted to him."

"Well, sure, that makes a whole lot of sense," said Arnie. "It's always a lot more pleasant being around people you can't stand."

"Well, it is. I feel like I can be myself when I'm around people I don't like. You know, you're not trying to make a good impression on them."

"You know what, Jas? Sometimes you're off the wall."

"I knew you wouldn't understand."

"Are you honestly trying to tell me that you were trying to make a good impression on Harry? That you've ever tried? Correct me if I'm wrong, but do you really think standing on his ledge and pushing Capetto out of his wheelchair were guaranteed to make a good impression on Harry?"

"That's different. On those occasions I was on the job. I'm talking about socially."

"Okay, let's talk socially. On those occasions when you've seen Harry and you haven't directly been on the job, have you ever told him the truth about anything?"

"You're supposed to be my friend, Arnie."

"I'm trying to be your friend. And I'm telling you, as a friend, that he's a really nice guy and he deserves better than you."

"I can't believe you said that, Arnie."

"Maybe I worded that wrong."

Chapter Six

Jas showed up at nine o'clock sharp for her appointment with Kingsley, only to find that first thing in the morning with Kingsley meant eight, not nine. A harried Teddy met her outside of the King's office.

"Uh, one thing, Ms. Rafferty, before you go in."

"I'm already late," said Jas.

"I just wanted to warn you. Last time you saw Mr. Kingsley you corrected him."

"I beg your pardon?"

"When he called you a detective. You corrected him."

"I said I was an investigator."

Teddy beamed. "That's right, you do remember."

"So what's the point?" asked Jas.

"No one corrects the King."

"The King?"

"That's what we call him."

"And no one corrects him?"

"Not to my knowledge," said Teddy. "The King doesn't like being corrected. The King is always right."

"Maybe for you—you work for him."

"May I remind you, Ms. Rafferty, your agency is also working for him. Please don't take it amiss; I just thought I'd warn you, that's all."

"Okay, I'm warned."

"You were also impertinent, although I must say you do it well."

"Well, thanks, I guess," said Jas, walking through the door that Teddy was opening for her.

She caught the King with a cruller halfway to his mouth. Since it had always been her theory that fat people ate in secret, she expected him to try to hide the cruller, but instead it made its way into his already open mouth. All of it.

Without waiting for an invitation, Jas took the chair facing Kingsley and sat down. She got her written report out of her knapsack and placed it on the desk in front of a plate holding several more crullers. They all looked disgustingly fattening. Jas longed to snatch one for herself but prided herself on the fact that she had self-control.

"What's that?" asked the King, his mouth encrusted with sugar.

"My report," said Jas.

"I'd prefer to hear an oral report."

That somehow didn't surprise her. Anyone who shoveled in food the way he did had to have some kind of oral fixation. "There's not much to report, sir. The subject in question is a legal tenant."

"And?"

"And what?"

"And what else did you find out?"

"Nothing."

"Then what are you doing here?"

"You asked me to report in."

The King reached for another cruller and eyed it with more lust than Jas had ever been eyed by a man. "What's your next step?"

"I'm not sure yet," said Jas, no inspiration coming to mind.

"I suggest you bug his apartment."

"I suggest you see too many spy movies," said Jas, and saw a stricken Teddy frenziedly shaking his head at her.

"Are you implying that your agency is not equipped to bug someone's apartment?"

"Sir, what you're asking for is a full-time operation. Planting bugs wouldn't be a difficulty, but it would necessitate someone, close by, listening in at all hours."

"I expect a full-time operation," said the King.

"I doubt whether Stanley will go for that."

"Stanley will go for whatever I tell Stanley to go for. Stanley is now working for me."

Jas didn't like the sound of this at all. "Well, I don't see how it can be done. What do you expect me to do, park a van across the street from his apartment and sit in it night and day?"

"That's a possibility," said the King, "but I have a better suggestion. There happens to be one vacant apartment in Mr. Keyes's building. I shall make it available to you. That way you won't even have to commute to work."

"But he'll see me going in and out of the building," said Jas.

"What if he does? He doesn't know you; he won't know you're a detective—"

"A private investigator."

"It'll be the perfect arrangement. I'd like you to start immediately. You have the key for her, Teddy?"

Teddy's hand was shaking as he handed her the key.

"Any questions, Ms. Rafferty?" asked the King.

"I think a man might be better for this job."

"Nonsense. I pride myself on being an equal-opportunity employer."

Jas got up, wondering how in the world she was going to pull this off. "I'll get started on it, sir."

"And I'll want daily reports. By telephone, of course."

"Yes, sir."

Kingsley leaned forward, dropping crumbs all over his desk. "Can I interest you in a cruller?"

Feeling very virtuous, she said, "No, thank you."

"Perhaps a few Godiva chocolates?"

"No, thanks."

"A Malomar?"

"No."

"Nothing?"

Jas shook her head.

The King sighed, scattering the crumbs. "Show her out, Teddy."

"THERE'S SOMETHING about her I like, Teddy," mused the King.

"She seems efficient," said Teddy.

"Really? I didn't notice that."

"You're right, of course," said Teddy. "I didn't notice it, either."

"No, it's a certain spirit she has. You know what it is, Teddy? She stands up to me. No one around here ever stands up to me. Everyone kowtows, agrees with my every word, but are they sincere? I think not. One day I'll have an employee who has the guts to stand up to me, to disagree with me, and then I'll know I've found my crown prince. I think I'd like a few more crullers, Teddy. Will you see that someone gets them for me?''

"Don't you think you've had enough?'' asked Teddy.

"What did you say?''

"I was just trying to stand up to you, sir,'' said Teddy, practically shaking in his shoes.

"Try that again, Teddy, and you're fired.''

"Yes, sir. Of course, sir. I'll get on those crullers right away.''

HARRY WAS TAKING a taxi through the Times Square area when he spotted the billboard. He literally could not believe his eyes.

"Stop,'' he said to the driver.

"You crazy, man? I can't stop here.''

"Stop the cab. I want to get out.''

"I can't even get near the curb,'' said the driver, who was now trying to cut off everyone between them and the curb and was getting a lot of irate drivers honking at him, none of them giving an inch.

"I've got to get out here,'' said Harry, taking a ten-dollar bill out of his pocket and waving it in front of the driver's face.

"Why didn't you say so, buddy?'' said the driver, swerving across the traffic and ending up with two wheels on the curb.

Harry got out of the cab and stood there looking at the billboard. It wasn't the large letters that bothered him, though they didn't exactly make his day. Still, there wasn't anything he could really object to in "You don't have to be a fat cat to shop at Kingsley's. In fact, it helps if you aren't." What he objected to was the fat cat pictured.

He found the nearest working phone booth and called his lawyer.

"Mel, isn't Grogan copyrighted?"

"Sure thing, Harry. Has been since you started."

"Well, listen, Mel—Kingsley now has a billboard in Times Square." Harry described what it looked like.

"You saying he's using Grogan?"

"Not exactly. He's a lot fatter than Grogan, but he's certainly recognizable."

"That's it? Just fatter?"

"Well, you know that mustache Grogan has?"

"Yeah, of course. A cute mustache."

"Well, it's no longer cute. In fact, it makes him look a lot like Adolf Hitler."

"That's bad news, Harry."

"You're telling me?"

"I'll work on getting an injunction on it for copyright infringement."

"I want that billboard down. It makes Grogan look like an evil dictator."

"I'll see what I can do, Harry. Give me a call this afternoon and I'll let you know what's happening."

Harry, who in his youth had filled in his share of mustaches on the famous and not-so-famous faces on billboards, felt very much like climbing up to this particular billboard and removing the mustache. He realized the irony in it but still didn't like it. No one was going to mess with Grogan and get away with it.

"HEY, JAS," yelled Charlie as she passed by his office on the way to see Stanley. "Come in here a minute."

Jas paused in his doorway. "Good morning, Charlie."

"Come here," said Charlie, motioning for her to come closer.

Jas edged closer to his desk, expecting one of Charlie's jokes. "What do you want?"

"I wanted to warn you, that's all. I was afraid if you weren't warned, you'd laugh."

"Get to the point, Charlie."

"Stanley got a rug."

"Why didn't he just carpet the whole office?"

Charlie became convulsed with laughter. "Not that kind of rug, Jas—one for his head. Ever see any pictures of the Beatles when they were young?"

Jas nodded.

"That's what Stanley looks like. I'm just trying to help you out. Marlene laughed when she saw him and was almost fired on the spot."

"I don't think I'll laugh," said Jas. "I'm not in a laughing mood."

She was wrong, though. It took all the self-possession she could summon not to laugh at the sight of Stanley with thick, dark bangs across his forehead. He didn't look like one of those before-and-after pictures where the formerly bald man suddenly looks ten years younger. He looked like someone with a modern, evolved face and a caveman head of hair.

"Did you see Kingsley?" asked Stanley.

"I think he's off the wall, Stanley. He wants us to bug Harry Keyes's apartment."

"We're investigators, Jas. It's not off the wall for investigators to do that. It's part of the job."

"Stanley, he expects me to move into an empty apartment he has in Keyes's building and monitor his every sound night and day."

"It'll keep you off the streets."

"I like the streets."

"Come on, Jas, that doesn't sound so bad. We can have food sent up to you. And you already know him, so it shouldn't be difficult to get invited into his apartment and place the bugs."

"What if I never hear anything incriminating? I could spend the rest of my life there waiting in vain."

"Give it a week, Jas. If you don't get anything on him in a week, we'll try something else. Think of it as a week's vacation on the Upper West Side."

"Just what I always wanted."

"Go home and pack what you'll need. I'll get Charlie to set up the equipment for you, and when you get up there he'll show you how to use it."

"I had that in school."

"He'll give you a refresher course."

"I don't need—"

"You're treading on thin ice, Rafferty. If you screw this one up..."

Jas stood up. "All right. And, Stanley, I like your new hairstyle."

Stanley gave her a dubious look as though assessing her sincerity. When she didn't change her expression, he said, "Thanks. It's amazing the difference a blow dryer makes, isn't it?"

Jas left the office before she burst out laughing.

HARRY WAS DOODLING. Sometimes his doodling turned into successful strips. Sometimes it remained doodling. Today it was turning into visual invective against Kingsley that wasn't good for anything besides venting Harry's anger.

When the knock came at his door he was glad of an excuse to get up from the drawing table. He was getting nowhere and probably would not get anywhere until he heard from his lawyer.

He opened the door to one of his neighbors, the one, Harry recalled, who was considering taking the money and moving to New Jersey.

"Come on in," said Harry.

"I don't want to disturb you."

"You're not, believe me. What's the problem?"

"I don't know if you caught my name at the meeting, but it's Lyle," said the young man, holding out his hand.

Harry shook it. "Is this about the building going co-op?"

Lyle nodded. "You remember those letters we were all sent? The ones where the Kingsley Corporation asked us to call and you advised us to ignore?"

"I remember."

"I called," said Lyle. "I wanted to see what they were offering."

"What happened?"

"They said if I wanted to stay I could buy my apartment for a hundred and eighty thousand dollars."

"How big is it?" asked Harry, curious as to how much his would go for."

Lyle looked around. "It's a studio—about half the size of your living room."

"The man's got a gold mine here if he can get those prices."

"His co-ops are all going for prices like that. I've been checking them out in the *Times*."

"Are you thinking of buying?"

"That's just not possible," said Lyle. "My rent's six hundred a month now and I can barely manage that."

"Did they make you any kind of offer?"

"Yeah. Eighteen thousand in cash if I move out right away. They said the longer I put it off, the less they'll pay me."

"If you want to take the cash and run," said Harry, "do it. Don't feel obligated to the tenants' association."

"I've never had that much money at one time in my life," said Lyle. "Of course, I realize it wouldn't get me another apartment in the city, but I figure I can look around in New Jersey, and even after the two months' rent and security I'll have to pay over there, I'll have enough left over for a car."

"You might as well go for it."

"On the other hand," said Lyle, "what I keep thinking is, what if you win? What if you force Kingsley not to go co-op? If I had the choice, I'd rather stay here. I've been here seven years and it's home, you know what I mean?"

Harry knew exactly what he meant. He might not like what was happening to the neighborhood, but he still loved his apartment and its proximity to the park. "I don't know what to tell you, Lyle. But realistically, I don't think we'll be able to do more than prolong the inevitable."

"I thought maybe I'd think about it for a few days and maybe we could have another tenants' meeting."

"Sure, I'll set one up. How about tomorrow night in my apartment?"

"Great. I saw that ad on TV this morning, and I wanted to tell you, I think your comic strip has a lot more class than Kingsley's ads."

"What ad?"

"The one with the fat Grogan with the evil-looking mustache lurking outside of Kingsley's."

"On TV?"

Lyle nodded. "I thought you knew about it."

"I saw the billboard. I haven't seen it on TV."

"I know you'll get him, Harry—we're all cheering for you."

"This time I'm going for the jugular."

THE DOODLING TOOK ON definition. There was Grogan, turning into the familiar door of his apartment building. There were his neighbors, cats of all sizes and descriptions, milling around the lobby with downcast faces. There was the reason for their distress: a sign proclaiming that Kingsley had bought their building and it was now going co-op.

The military skirmish was going to turn into a fullfledged war.

JAS HAD ALWAYS WANTED to do exactly what she now was being forced to do by Kingsley, and yet now she didn't particularly want to do it. As a child she had loved to spy on people, to listen in on telephone conversations and to find out other people's secrets. To do it to Harry, though, seemed like a betrayal. At the very least, it didn't seem like the right way to start off a relationship. Or even a friendship, for that matter.

On the way home to pack, she stopped by Arnie's messenger service. It appeared to be a slow day; several of the messengers, including Arnie, were sitting around playing cards.

She walked over to the table and looked over Arnie's shoulder. "Can I talk to you, Arnie?"

"In a minute, Jas. I've got a great hand."

That was all it took for the others to fold, and Arnie, winking at Jas, said, "Great bluff. We ought to try that more often."

They walked outside and stood leaning against the building. "I have to move out for a few days," said Jas. "I just wanted to let you know so you wouldn't worry."

"What's happening?"

"I've got to bug Harry's apartment. Kingsley's letting me use a vacant apartment in Harry's building. The problem is, Kingsley doesn't know I know Harry. What am I going to do, Arnie? Harry's bound to catch me going in or out of the building at some point."

"Why should he catch you? The beauty of it is you'll know all his moves in advance. It'll be like you're right there in the apartment with him."

"I hadn't thought of that."

"Sure. I mean, if you hear him on the phone making a date with some woman for eight o'clock, you'll know there'll be some safe time when you can move around."

"You think he dates, Arnie?"

"I would imagine so. There didn't seem to be anything wrong with him."

"You think women are attracted to him?"

"Well, I can't speak as a woman, but you're attracted to him, aren't you?"

"I was hoping I was the only one."

"Since when were you afraid of a little competition? Anyway, you'll have the advantage. You're going to get to know him intimately."

"He'd really hate me for this, you know."

Arnie nodded. "I know I would. What we're talking about here is invading his privacy. On television you need a court order to do that."

"That's when it's law-enforcement agencies. We're private."

"That makes it all right?"

"Arnie, what I don't need right now is a lecture on ethics. You think I feel great about this?"

"Well, at some point, Jas, I think you're going to have to choose between Harry and your job."

"I don't want to hear that," said Jas. "I thought that was the kind of choice women didn't have to make anymore."

Arnie said, "I believe the choice women don't have to make these days is between having a husband and children and having a career."

"Not between a job and a relationship?"

"No."

"What's the difference?" asked Jas.

"I'm not really sure."

"Well, it sounds the same to me."

"Maybe you're right," said Arnie. "But that's in general and this is personal. And on a personal level I can't see Harry going for a detective."

"An investigator."

"That, either."

"You're wrong, Arnie, dead wrong. I would think he'd be relieved to find out I'm an investigator rather than some nut who wants to kill herself. Or someone who tries to kill old men in wheelchairs."

"Maybe you're right. But anyway, keep in touch. And if you get bored, just give me a call."

"Thanks, Arnie."

WHEN JAS ARRIVED at the apartment, she found a one-bedroom furnished with sound equipment and Charlie and nothing else. There wasn't even a refrigerator.

"What am I supposed to do, Charlie, sleep on the floor? Work on the floor? This is ridiculous."

"I've been on worse stakeouts," said Charlie.

"Name one."

"Central Park in the rain."

"Name another."

"I was supposed to be a bum in Grand Central once. Try that sometime and see what it does for your self-image."

Jas sat down on the floor beside Charlie while he showed her how to work the equipment. "I feel like a prisoner," she said. "I'm going to be afraid to ever leave in case he sees me."

"Your first mistake was getting friendly with him."

"Give me a break, Charlie. I was out on the ledge. I wasn't trying to strike up a conversation with him."

"You're going to have to use a disguise, that's all."

"He's seen all my disguises."

"Well, I can't help you out with that. But I can bring over an air mattress you can use."

"Thanks."

"Although you could go for the bandaged face."

"What?"

"My mother got a face peel; you know, one of those things that removes wrinkles. Anyway, when she went home she had her whole face bandaged and the security guard in her building wouldn't let her in because he didn't recognize her."

"I think I'll pass on that one."

Charlie reached into his shirt pocket and handed her six small metal disks. "You want me to help you plant these?"

Jas shook her head. "I'll get myself invited over and do it."

"How're you going to manage that?"

"I'll think of something."

"Well, listen, be sure to get the phones. And one under the bed's always a good idea."

"I know where they're supposed to go."

"And don't forget the bathroom."

"Charlie, there is no way I'm going to plant one in the bathroom. This isn't Al Capone we're going after. This is a nice man who Kingsley's got it in for. I personally think the whole thing is a complete waste of time."

"You'll get overtime, you know, maybe even triple time."

"Really?"

Charlie grinned at her. "Sure, you're going to be working twenty-four hours a day, aren't you?"

"I hadn't thought of that."

Charlie stood up. "See, you look cheered up already." He started to put on his wrinkled trenchcoat, then changed his mind and handed it to her. "Here, take this. You can wear it with that felt fedora of yours. If you run into Keyes on the street, just fall into the gutter and you'll be an instant bum. New Yorkers never even notice derelicts in the gutter."

Jas stood up and tried it on. The bottom of the coat hit the floor and the sleeves hung down past her knees. "This is perfect, Charlie," she said.

"You got your hat with you?"

She reached into her satchel and produced it. Charlie set it on her head, then pulled the hat down and the collar of the raincoat up. "Now scrunch down. Remember, bums never have good posture."

Jas scrunched down and put her hands in the pockets.

"Perfect," said Charlie. "You can wear that on the streets at night and even your own mother wouldn't recognize you."

HARRY AND PHILLY had been in the park throwing a football around. About once a week they got together to play a little ball. It made them feel as though they were kids again and playing hooky from school. Now they were on their way back to Harry's place and were

just crossing Columbus Avenue when Philly said,
"Isn't that your friend Jas over there?"

"Over where?" Harry asked.

"Across the street from your place."

Harry lowered his glasses for a better look. "I
wonder what she's doing in this neighborhood."

"Harry, my friend, she's obviously got it bad. Now
she's hanging around your neighborhood in the hope
of seeing you."

"At least she's not back on the ledge."

"Oh-oh, look at that. Now she's moving, acting
casual, walking along in our direction as though that
had been her intention all the time."

"She's on the other side of the street."

"What do you want to bet she crosses over? And
then pretends to be surprised when she sees us."

"There's got to be an explanation for this."

"Why don't you come right out and ask her what
she's doing lurking around your neighborhood?"

"I can't do that, Philly—it'd just embarrass her."

"So what are you going to do?"

"Invite her up for a drink."

"Great. Maybe she'll tell me her sign this time."

"Not you, Philly. You I expect to disappear."

"But I'll hear about it later, right?"

"Right."

Philly said, "There she goes, right on time, crossing the street and still pretending she doesn't see us.
She really thinks she's putting one over on you. How
does it feel to be relentlessly pursued, Harry?"

"Right now I'm enjoying it."

Chapter Seven

Jas felt like a total fool.

She knew Harry and his friend had spotted her. The problem was she had been watching his building with the idea that he'd either come out of the front door or come from the direction of Broadway, and so she hadn't kept an eye on the remaining direction.

And she called herself an investigator?

Too late she had seen them, and she was sure they had seen her. And what they must have seen was her standing across the street doing nothing. She decided that if push came to shove, she would admit that she had been waiting for him, that she had been on a job interview in the area and since she had been so close, she thought she'd buy him a drink if he was interested.

What was lucky was that he hadn't even questioned her being in the area. And before she could come up with her excuse, he had invited her to his place for a drink. That was perfect. That was just what she had wanted. Because if they had gone out for a drink, then she would have had to think up an excuse to go home with him for a while, and the only reason for going home with a guy instead of staying in a bar was to get to know him better in a way that she felt was totally premature.

Having sex with Harry at this point wasn't even under consideration. She might be attracted, but she barely knew him. What's more, it would be taking advantage of him because he would think he was with someone else entirely. It would almost certainly confuse things. It would be consorting with the enemy, even though she had a hard time conceiving of Harry as the enemy.

By the time they walked up to the sixth floor, Jas was counting the one blessing she could think of relating to the job, and that was that the empty apartment she was in was on the fourth floor and a much easier walk.

"What'll you have?" asked Harry as he engaged the multiple locks on the door.

"A beer's fine."

"No gin?"

"That was to calm my nerves," she told him. "My nerves are okay today."

Harry went into the kitchen and Jas walked over to the drawing table, where the real Grogan was spread out on top of the latest comic strip. When she got within a foot of him, Grogan hissed. He didn't seem to like her for some reason. Maybe he knew she was up to no good.

The telephone was on a filing cabinet that sat next to the drawing table, along with mugs filled with freshly sharpened pencils. Jas picked up the phone. She slipped her hand into her pocket and then slid the bugging device under the phone in one smooth movement. Just as swiftly it dropped off the phone and onto the floor. She tried it again, this time turning the disk over, and this time it stuck. Grogan made a big production of moving around so that his back was to her, all the while swishing his tail.

Jas looked around for a metal surface to attach another one to, but couldn't find a likely spot except for the TV. She finally shoved one under the couch. If Harry was anything like her, he wouldn't move the couch until such time as he either moved or bought a new one. Unless he was the type to actually vacuum under his couch. She didn't think that was possible. She couldn't possibly be attracted to the kind of person who would vacuum under furniture.

She wandered out to the kitchen just as he was leaving it with two cans of beer under one arm and a bowl of potato chips in his other hand.

"Could I have a glass of water?" Jas asked.

"Sure, help yourself. The glasses are over the sink and there's ice in the freezer."

He continued down the hall and she went into the kitchen, saw another telephone and bugged that, plus the refrigerator. In the unlikely event Harry talked to his ice-cube trays, she'd hear every word. Unless the disks stopped working if they froze. She couldn't remember Charlie saying anything about that. Before leaving the kitchen, she poured herself a glass of water and dumped it down the sink. She thought that was a professional touch just in case Harry was listening to hear whether she was actually getting herself a glass of water.

She decided to forget about the bedroom. Like the bathroom, she decided it was the kind of place where he should be assured of privacy. And if what went on in his bedroom was more of a sharing experience than a solitary one, she didn't want to hear it.

Harry was on his drawing stool and Grogan was on the couch when she got back to the living room. Neither of them moved when she entered. Harry appeared to be deep in thought and Grogan was so still he could have been the work of a taxidermist. Then in a second Harry noticed her and smiled, and Grogan, as she took a seat on the couch, catapulted onto the floor and collapsed under the coffee table.

"Your cat doesn't like me," said Jas, but it didn't bother her as she wasn't overly fond of cats. She liked the comic strip Grogan, but then, that Grogan was an extension of Harry's mind. The real Grogan seemed nothing more than an overfed, overly domesticated animal. She preferred her animals in the wild, or at least out of the city.

"Grogan doesn't like anyone," said Harry. "He only tolerates me because I feed him."

"Then why feed him?"

He looked surprised at the question. "You're talking about my inspiration. Before I met Grogan, I was peddling unsalable strips that no one wanted."

"What do you mean, met him?"

"He showed up on my balcony one day, rather like you did, since I assumed he came by way of the ledge and didn't just materialize."

"And he stayed?"

"Not at first," said Harry. "He'd show up every so often, but I'm pretty sure he was living with someone else. Then I offered him some of my pizza one day and right after that he moved in with me. Since he's twice as big now as he was before, I assume he prefers the food here. Or maybe he doesn't, but I don't let him out anymore so he's pretty much forced to live here."

"Better not offer me any pizza, Harry," said Jas, making a joke, but Harry didn't laugh. "I was only kidding," she said when the silence began to stretch. She took a sip of her beer and stretched her legs out so that they were under the coffee table. Grogan, without even opening his eyes, rolled away from her feet.

Harry looked bemused. "Now I don't know what to do because suddenly I have an overwhelming urge for a pizza."

Jas made a slight move as if to get up. "Maybe I should go and leave you to your dinner." She had no real intention of going, though. Surely it would be easier and more comfortable to monitor Harry from the vantage point of his couch than to go downstairs, where all she had was an air mattress that didn't hold air very well.

"Finish your beer first," said Harry. "I don't eat this early anyway. Would you mind, though, if I put on the Channel 4 news?"

"Of course not," said Jas. It made her uncomfortable, though, when he got up and turned on the TV. Except for ball games, she always thought of television watching as something best done alone.

Bored by the news, she found her eyes drawn to the movement below her, where she saw Grogan's paw moving. He was still in a reclining position and it might have been a twitch, but his paw was making almost a sweeping motion and what it appeared to be sweeping was the area under the couch where she had planted the bug. And she was very definitely getting paranoid.

When Harry said, "I'll be damned," Jas looked up in time to see a very strange commercial. "Wasn't that Grogan?" she asked Harry, but before she had even finished asking, the Kingsley logo was on the screen.

"I heard about it, but that's the first time I've seen it," said Harry.

"I hadn't known about that," said Jas.

"No reason why you should. It just started today. He also has a billboard down in Times Square."

"With Grogan on it?"

"Close enough, yes, but didn't you notice the difference?"

"It looked exactly like Grogan to me," said Jas.

"He didn't look evil?"

Jas shrugged. "I only saw it for a second."

"I called my lawyer today and he's getting an injunction against Kingsley. Grogan's copyrighted."

"But you used his department store in your strip—what's the difference?"

"There's a big difference."

"What exactly?"

"Well, if you can't see it, there's no way I can explain it to you."

Grogan was suddenly up on his feet and batting something around on the floor. "What's he got?" Harry asked.

"Probably a bug," said Jas, almost laughing at her play on words. Then as Harry got up to see, she began to get nervous, but by the time Harry got over to where Grogan seemed to have it cornered, the cat snatched at it with his teeth.

Jas watched as Harry tried to pry open the cat's jaws. Then she saw Grogan swallow and wondered if she was going to have to listen to his heartbeat all night.

Harry shook his head and sat back down, this time at the other end of the couch. "That cat'll eat anything."

"So are you going to retaliate?" asked Jas.

"You mean not feed him?"

"No, I mean against Kingsley."

Harry smiled. "It's already in the works. And I don't mean the injunction."

"What're you going to go after this time, his airline?"

Harry shook his head. "I'm going after what I should've gone after to begin with. I really had nothing against his department store. What I do object to is his buying up half the apartment houses in the city and making them co-ops so that all of my friends are being forced to move out of Manhattan. What we're going to end up with is a city where the poorest people are the upper middle-class."

"I don't think a comic strip is going to stop him," said Jas, thinking of the fat despot in his tower suite.

Grogan walked over and stood in front of the coffee table and then, as though he had choreographed it, began a series of heaves.

"Is he having a fit?" asked Jas.

"No, he's getting ready to throw up. Usually it's a fur ball, but this time I think it was the bug that didn't agree with him."

Great timing, Jas silently congratulated the cat.

With one final heave, the cat's mouth opened and something shiny flew out of it and ricocheted off the coffee table.

Harry got up and reached down to pick it up. "This is strange," he said.

Jas was thinking it might be the shortest stakeout in history.

Harry sat back down, examining the disk that lay in the palm of his hand. "Have you ever seen anything like this?" he asked Jas.

Jas pretended to study it. "It looks like a part of a computer," she said.

"Really? What part?"

"I'm not sure what you call it."

"But I don't have a computer."

"It was only a guess."

Harry was up now and walking over to his stereo. "Maybe it fell off this. It looks high tech, whatever it is."

She was worried that the disk was going to be the topic of conversation from then on, but instead, Harry put it on top of the stereo, turned off the TV and sat back down on the couch.

"So you don't think Grogan can defeat Kingsley?" he asked her.

"I don't see how. I don't believe it's illegal to turn buildings co-op."

"No, but the way he often does it is."

"He offers people money to move out, doesn't he?"

"Don't you read the papers, Jas?"

"I read the comic strips. And the sports pages. Sometimes a movie review."

...be tempted!

See inside for special
4 FREE BOOKS offer

 Harlequin American Romance

"Kingsley has been charged, numerous times, with forcing people out of buildings by turning off the heat and water. On a couple of occasions he's been suspected of burning down buildings when he couldn't get permits to tear them down and rebuild."

"Then why isn't he in jail?"

"He should be," said Harry, "but his lawyers always get him out of it."

"You're not an investigative reporter, Harry; you draw comic strips."

"Human nature's a funny thing. People will read about a building suspiciously burning down, but if they don't live in the building they don't give it a second thought. But for some reason, they take Grogan pretty seriously. You should have seen the mail I got when I went after Kingsley's Department Store."

"You get fan mail?"

"Not me. The mail is addressed to Grogan."

"You better watch it or Kingsley will decide to buy up all the newspapers and put you out of business."

HARRY COULDN'T FIGURE her out.

If she was going after him, as Philly thought, then why was she giving him such a hard time? Why wasn't she saying things like, "Oh, I know you can do it, Harry," and, "Oh, what a darling cat you have." Why was she acting as though she couldn't care less? Not that he didn't prefer it this way, but why would she go to so much trouble to meet him and then not try to make a good impression? She was the most confusing person he had ever met.

Pursuing him had a sexual connotation to it, didn't it? She was a woman, he was a man, and if she were as eager to get to him as she appeared to be, then sex had to be part of it. Wasn't sex what groupies were all about? It stood to reason. He had done a little pursuing, but she had done more, and he had sex in mind. Not immediately, of course. But if he continued to see her, ultimately he would put it to the test. He wasn't asexual, after all. He hadn't been "fixed" as Grogan had been.

And yet—and he was about to make an experiment to test this theory—he was certain that what she had in mind was not sex. Or even affection. And yet she sat there, only inches away from him, and didn't act as though she would prefer to be anywhere else.

In a purely experimental way, he shifted a bit on the couch and spread his arm along the back of it. He could see her tense. Of course, the tensing might be in expectation, but he didn't think so. He somehow got the feeling that she wasn't sitting there willing him to make a move so that she could melt into his arms. It was a nice thought, but he didn't buy it.

He leaned forward to lift his beer can and, in doing so, allowed his arm to brush the back of her head. As he took a sip of the beer, he felt her head move away from his arm. He could hardly consider that preparatory to melting into his arms.

So what was the story? She ran up six flights of steep stairs just to get his autograph; she risked her life by perching on his ledge in the hope of seeing him and perhaps getting to know him; she hung around outside his building and jumped at the invitation to come in for a drink. All that for what? What did she hope to get out of it?

"Would you like another beer?" he asked her.

"I wouldn't mind."

Okay, so she was getting a couple of free beers. She was meeting her hero in person. No, there was no way he saw himself as anyone's hero. Maybe Grogan could be considered heroic, but not himself. So she loved his comic strip. Then why didn't she like the real Grogan? Why wasn't she making a fuss over him or at least giving him a pat on the head? Why wasn't she asking Harry where he got his ideas, which was the first question fans usually asked him? Why, in fact, was she looking bored?

He took the empty beer cans and went to the kitchen. He was thinking pizza would go pretty well with the beer. He stuck his head out of the kitchen and said, "I'm going to order up a pizza. That okay with you?"

"No anchovies," she said.

"Wrong. Grogan gets the anchovies."

He found himself wanting her to leave so that he could call Philly and ask him what the hell he thought was going on, because it was for damn sure he couldn't figure it out. At least he didn't think she was suicidal anymore. He was now pretty certain that standing on his ledge had been another ploy to meet him. Unless the whole thing had been scouting attempts to find a suicide spot, in which case... He stuck his head around the door again, but she was still on the couch. And then there was the guy in the wheelchair. That didn't fit into any theory at all.

He called in the order for the pizza, then took out two more beers. "So, tell me about yourself, Jas," he said, realizing that all he really knew about her was that she was a computer programmer and not too stable emotionally if she went to these lengths to meet men. He never would've figured computer people to be so emotional.

"What do you want to know?"

"Your hopes, your dreams, your fears, your desires." He had meant it as a joke but it came out making him sound like some idiotic fool in a singles bar. He revised it to, "I don't know—anything you want to tell me."

She got up and walked over to his drawing table, pretending to look at the new strip but not fooling him at all. She didn't want any more moves made on her; that was it.

Finally she said, "I'm an only child."

He thought in frames, rather like a comic strip. In the first frame was the only child, sitting apart from her parents with no one to play with. In the second frame she was being given a computer as a birthday present. The last frame showed her all alone in her room working at her computer while outside, groups of children were playing.

"I'll bet a lot of computer nuts are only children," he said.

"Why would you think that?"

"Well, it's kind of a solitary occupation, isn't it?"

"So is drawing comic strips."

"Okay, that proves it. I'm an only child, too. When other kids were outside playing ball, I was in my room drawing pictures."

"I was out playing ball," said Jas.

"I lied. I was out playing ball, too."

"Actually, I wanted to play for the Mets before I wanted to work with computers," she said.

"Okay, so you had a normal childhood. You weren't lonely, you weren't abused. I imagine you had friends."

"You're beginning to sound like your shrink friend. Next you'll be asking me my sign."

"I call it trying to get to know you. You want to hear about my childhood?"

"Not particularly."

"You don't think you're affected every day of your life by what happened to you in your childhood?"

She chuckled. "No."

"Neither do I," said Harry.

They were comparing notes on their respective high schools in Queens when the pizza was delivered. Harry took it into the kitchen to pick off the anchovies and put them in Grogan's bowl, then carried it into the living room with two more beers.

"That looks good," said Jas. "I forgot to eat lunch today."

"Why didn't you say you were starving?"

"I didn't know I was." She reached into the box and took a piece of pizza, and for a few minutes they ate in companionable silence. Harry tried to figure out what to do next.

For some reason, it didn't feel like a date. Nor did it feel like a couple of friends sitting around talking. What it felt was uncomfortable, as though she were just killing time before something more interesting happened, and he just happened to be the one she was killing time with.

Did he need this? No. But for some perverse reason he was still attracted to her. In order to shake her up and get some reaction out of her, he said, "What do you say we make out after we're finished eating?"

She laughed.

"You find that idea ludicrous?"

"You sound exactly like the average high-school boy from Queens."

"I was the average high-school boy from Queens."

"We're out of high school now, Harry."

"I was just trying to get a rise out of you."

"Why?"

"Because I can't figure you out, Jas, that's why."

"Like what am I doing here drinking your beer and eating your pizza if I don't want to go to bed with you?"

"Like what are you doing here at all?"

"You invited me."

"I invited you because you happened to be hanging around my block."

"I was hanging around your block because I was hoping to see you. It seems as though you only see me in weird situations and I wanted you to know that I'm usually a pretty normal person."

"Sex is pretty normal," he said, wondering what had gotten into him. That wasn't at all the kind of thing he usually said to a woman.

She reached for her second slice of pizza. "I need to know a man far better than I know you before I feel like having sex with him."

"What would you like to know about me?"

"You know, Harry, I get the feeling that if I started coming on strong, you'd back away."

She was reading him better than he was reading her. "I'm rather the same way," said Harry, "about getting to know someone better first. But there's something about you that makes me think it'd be impossible to really get to know you."

She looked pleased. "You find me a woman of mystery?"

"More like a Rubik's Cube."

SHE WAS BORING HIM to death. She could feel it, but she couldn't do anything about it. Here she was in one of the most fascinating of professions, one that was depicted in books and movies and on television and that everyone seemed to enjoy vicariously, and she couldn't even tell him about it. Instead of keeping him enthralled with her own personal detective stories, she had to act like the most boring of people, an unemployed computer programmer, which might, of course, prove to be the kind of profession that had its own interesting stories to tell. But since she wasn't even a real one, she didn't even have that to talk about.

And Harry seemed much too nice to ask her questions he was no doubt dying to ask her, such as why she had been contemplating jumping from his ledge, and why she shoved people in wheelchairs into the street, and why she was sitting in his living room drinking his beer and eating his pizza while at the same time not showing the proper amount of interest in him.

She was so very, very tempted to throw her arms around his neck, and kiss his tomato-smeared mouth, and tell him that if he'd just hang in there for a while the mystery would be cleared up and they could start fresh. He was so nice and meeting a nice man was such a novelty. Investigators weren't nice. The police she sometimes dealt with weren't nice. The people she investigated were far from nice. She had about despaired of ever meeting, let alone being attracted to, a nice man. And since he might very well be the only available one left in New York, she hated to have to continually confuse him, but she was glad that just this once she had had the chance to spend a normal evening with him.

It was an evening she had better bring to an end before any more lies had to be told. She finished her beer and said, "This has been great, Harry, but I better get home. I have to get up early for another job interview."

"It's only eight o'clock."

"I have to wash my hair and iron some clothes, stuff like that." She carried the empty pizza box out to the kitchen and washed her hands in the sink. When she finished he was standing at the door in his jacket.

"I'll walk you to the subway," he said.

"That's not necessary," she told him. "Anyway, I'll probably get a taxi."

She started to turn toward the door to let herself out and he put his hands on her shoulders and turned her back around to face him. He had the kind of look in his eyes that guys get when they're about to make a move. She tried to back up but she was right against the door. As his face moved closer she said, "No, Harry, that's not what I came up for."

"You didn't come up for pizza, either."

"Harry, I think you're doing this because you think it's expected of you. Well, I don't expect it, and I don't even think it's a very good idea."

"It's something I really want to do."

"Harry—" By the time she'd said it he was already kissing her. At first it didn't seem right to her. She was getting personal with the subject of one of her investigations, and that was a big no-no. But after about ten seconds it began to seem perfectly all right and, in fact, desirable. After twenty seconds she began to lose all interest in departing and wound her arms around Harry's neck. She began returning his kisses in earnest.

At the thirty-second mark Harry broke it off and smiled the happiest smile of all times. "There's something I really like about you, Jas."

She was afraid to ask him what. "Thanks for everything," she told him, meaning the beer, the pizza, the kiss. "You really don't have to go down with me."

"I insist. This neighborhood might look better than it used to, but it still has its share of muggers."

Unfortunately, it didn't look as though he meant to be dissuaded, so she followed him out of the apartment and down the stairs. Now she was actually going to have to get a cab.

He had just hailed a cab for her when he said, "I'll call you, all right? Maybe we could go out this weekend?"

"Sure," she said. "And thanks again."

"My pleasure."

Jas got into the taxi and said to the driver, "Go around the block, okay?"

"What're you, crazy, lady?"

"I'd like to go around the block."

"Why don't you walk around the block?"

"If I wanted to walk around the block I wouldn't have hailed a taxi. And since I don't see your off-duty lights on, I believe you're required to take me."

"It's your money."

"That's right, it is."

The driver raced around the block and it ended up costing her two dollars and fifty cents. And he wasn't at all happy to have to give her a receipt for the trip.

SITTING ON THE FLOOR with the earphones on, Jas heard footsteps, then the sound of water running, then some banging as though he were opening and closing cupboard doors. Then, very clearly, she heard Harry say, "You already ate, Grogan."

She felt incredibly sneaky. On the other hand, it was more entertaining than television. She wondered what Harry would say if he knew that instead of being whisked home in a taxi, she was two flights under him listening in to his private life. She had a feeling that whatever it was it wouldn't be complimentary. He might even be sorry he had kissed her.

She was already sorry he had kissed her. Because of that kiss she was feeling as though she'd like to join the enemy camp—in this case, Harry. She hated being Kingsley's pawn.

Poor Harry. If he still felt like seeing her after it was all over, she'd make it up to him by never lying to him again. At least about anything important. Maybe someday they'd laugh about this.

She heard a cat sound and Harry saying, "You don't want to go out there, Grogan. Come on, settle down. What's the matter, you didn't get your share of pizza? Thanks a lot, Grogan—do you always have to bite the hand that feeds you?"

Jas couldn't believe he was talking to his cat. Did he talk to his plants, too? Maybe his furniture? Why didn't he just turn on the TV so she could hear the ball game?

She was pretty sure he wasn't going to confide anything incriminating to his cat that Kingsley would want to hear, so she took off the headphones and went to the bathroom. When she returned and put them back on again, she thought at first he was still talking to Grogan.

Then she recognized Philly's voice saying, "You had pizza? That's it? Did you find out anything?"

"Yeah, I found out she was an only child."

"But not her sign, huh?"

"No, Philly, she doesn't seem to be forthcoming with her sign. Along with just about everything else."

"I figured she'd be spending the night. On the other hand, that might be too normal for her."

"I suggested it."

"And?"

"She laughed."

"I don't get it," said Philly. "She's lurking around your neighborhood waiting for you, then all she does is eat pizza and go home?"

"I kissed her."

"Ah. Now we get to the juicy part."

"Not juicy, Philly, just a kiss. And on her part it seemed more like a thank-you than a real kiss."

"And on your part?"

"I think I'm falling in love."

"Not again!"

"Come on, Philly, when was the last time I fell in love? It was two years ago."

"Two years and three months."

"She's the first woman who has really interested me in a long time."

"I think you're getting into being chased."

"I find it hard to believe that theory of yours, Philly. When we're alone, she really doesn't seem that interested in me."

"She's playing it cool."

"No, Philly, she's playing it indifferent."

"Then you come up with a better theory. But I'm telling you, I'll bet fans have done more bizarre things to get to know celebrities."

"Michael Jackson maybe, but not people who do comic strips."

"Anyway, it's worked, and you can't argue with success."

"What's worked?"

"She's gotten you to fall for her, hasn't she? I'd call that being pretty successful. I wonder what her next move will be."

"I said I'd call her."

"Did you ask her about the messenger getup?"

"I didn't want to embarrass her."

"You're too much, Harry. She impersonates a messenger to get your autograph, she shows up on your ledge in a phony suicide attempt, she tries to kill some old man in a wheelchair, she just happens to be hanging around in front of your building, and you're afraid of embarrassing her? I don't think you could embarrass her."

"Okay, it all sounds nutty, I agree. But you liked her, too. You know you did."

"Maybe you ought to investigate her."

"What?"

"Find out about her. For all you know, she might have escaped from the psychiatric ward of Bellevue."

"I couldn't do that, Philly."

"Why not?"

"Because it's an invasion of privacy. It's unethical. What kind of person would investigate someone he was interested in?"

"I don't mean you'd have to do it yourself. Hire one of those detective agencies. My father hired one to investigate the guy my sister married."

"Did they find out anything?"

"Nothing that stopped her from marrying him."

"Well, that's not for me. I think a relationship should be based on trust."

"Normally I would agree with you, Harry, but this thing between you and Jas has been anything but normal from the start."

"I'm going to get off and do some work, Philly. I just didn't want to keep you in suspense."

"I'm glad you did. This is better than *Dallas*."

"You still watch that garbage."

"I'm hooked, Harry. But I'm willing to miss it Friday if you want to catch the fights at the Garden."

"You're on."

"See you, Harry."

"See you, Philly."

Jas collapsed back on the air mattress feeling stupid, guilty and exhilarated, all at the same time.

She felt really stupid that Harry had recognized her as the messenger and thought she had gone through that and the ledge escapade just to meet him. The day she went through that much trouble to meet a man she'd give it up and join a nunnery.

She had never, ever, been attracted to celebrities. Well, maybe when she was a teenager, but certainly not since she'd been an adult. He wasn't a celebrity anyway—Grogan was the celebrity. How humiliating that he would think she was the kind of person who would fake a suicide attempt just to meet him. It made her feel like crawling under the mattress and never coming back out.

On top of that, she felt guilty. The guy was having genuine feelings about her and she was spying on him. She didn't think he was actually falling in love; it was a little early for that. But despite the fact that she must seem like an out-and-out nut to him, he really liked her.

What's more, she felt the same way about him. And here she was, finally in the position of meeting a guy she really liked, and what did she do about it? Lie to him. Spy on him. And then report back to the man who was out to ruin him. Talk about guilt.

And underneath the humiliation and the guilt there was the bottom layer of exhilaration that had been there ever since she kissed him. God, it had been ages since she felt like that about a man. She felt like dancing around the empty apartment and singing an aria from some wildly romantic opera. Except she was a klutz when it came to dancing and she didn't know any operas.

But why did he have to confide in Philly? And why did Philly have to give him advice like having her investigated? A mature man would keep those things to himself, wouldn't he? A mature man wouldn't immediately report in to his friend. After all, it wasn't any of Philly's business, was it?

She couldn't wait to tell Arnie.

THE KING WAS RECLINING on his satin chaise lounge and reading the preliminary report that the AAAAA Detective Agency had messengered over to him. He had deliberately not read it right away so that he'd have something to look forward to that evening.

He popped a piece of peppermint into his mouth and turned to the first page. He then proceeded to devour the pages with the same avidity as he devoured the bowl of candy.

It was only fair that he was having her investigated. She would know everything there was to know about him from all the magazine interviews and articles that had been written about him. Now he would get to know her equally well.

He thought about her all alone in the apartment he now owned. Was she thinking about him? Were her thoughts straying to him the way he kept finding his straying to her? Was she, perchance, fantasizing about him?

If only he didn't have a phobia about leaving his tower, he would go over and keep her company. But it was so comfortable here and she might not have any food in the place. He could wait. He would be patient. Very soon, if all went well, she would be sharing the tower with him.

He thought of sharing breakfast with her, and lunch. He pictured afternoon tea with delicious little sandwiches and pastries. He thought of long, elaborate dinners with sumptuous desserts, with Jas seated by his side. He thought of midnight snacks in his king-size bed. He thought of the two of them raiding the refrigerator in the middle of the night.

It all sounded so delectable.

Chapter Eight

Jas fell asleep with the earphones on. What awakened her was the sound of Harry's clock radio. A few minutes later she heard rattling sounds that appeared to be coming from his kitchen. Then there was silence for a good hour, during which time she got dressed.

When she was beginning to think he was going to stay home all day and she was going to starve to death, she heard the slamming of a door. She went to her own door and peeked outside, and, sure enough, she heard someone coming down the stairs. When she saw the top of Harry's head go by in the stairwell, she ran to the front window, lifted it and looked down at the sidewalk. Harry soon appeared, turning in the direction of the park.

Jas ran downstairs and out of the building, turning in the opposite direction from Harry and heading for Broadway, where she found a phone booth in order to report in.

"Investigator Rafferty reporting," she said when she got through to Kingsley.

"Yes?" he said, with the same kind of expectation in his voice that he had in his eyes when he was going after those crullers.

"Nothing to report, sir. The subject stayed at home last night and watched the Mets game."

"I'll bet you're a Mets fan, too," said Kingsley.

"As a matter of fact, I am."

"I was sure of it."

"Well, most New Yorkers are, I guess."

"On the contrary," said Kingsley. "I would imagine half of them are Yankee fans."

"I guess you're right," said Jas, wondering why Kingsley was engaging in small talk.

"That's all you have to report?"

"Well, there was a home run in the eighth with the bases loaded and—"

"I'm not interested in a replay of the ball game," she was told.

"Well, that's all that happened."

"Any telephone conversations?"

"One. It appeared to be to a friend of his, also male."

"Anything interesting?"

"Mostly they were talking about the home run in the eighth."

"I see. Tell me, Ms. Rafferty, do you have fond memories of Forest Hills?"

Jas felt herself tense. "Why do you ask that?"

There was a pause and then a chuckle. "Aren't you from Forest Hills?"

"I am, actually, but how did you know?"

"I picked it up from your accent."

"What accent?"

"People from Forest Hills have a distinctive accent. I pick up on it every time."

"That's news to me," said Jas. "I thought I had just a regular New York accent."

"It's a lovely accent, quite charming. Well, get back on the job and I'll expect to hear from you again tomorrow. I hope at that time you'll have something more interesting to report. And, Ms. Rafferty, would you care to have dinner with me Saturday night?"

"What did you say, sir?"

"No need to call me sir; you may call me King. I was extending an invitation to you to have dinner with me in my tower on Saturday night. I thought we'd start off with escargots, then perhaps venison steak with new potatoes, followed by—"

"Thank you, sir, uh, King, but I make it a practice never to mix business with pleasure."

"Well, perhaps at a later date then."

Not if she had anything to say about it, thought Jas as she hung up the phone.

HARRY HAD COME UPON some odd scenes in Central Park on different occasions, but nothing like what he was seeing now. The western shore of the lake appeared to be ringed with furniture. There was a living-room suite arranged on top of a rug; there was a kitchen table and chairs set beneath a tree; and under a tarpaulin, which was suspended between two other trees, was a bedroom set. There was even an occupant still in the bed.

He knew there were thousands of homeless people in the city. Indeed, it was hard not to be aware of them when they occupied every park bench and hundreds of doorways and were to be seen sleeping in the various subway and train stations. But those people, although they often had multiple shopping bags full of possessions and even the occasional shopping cart, never had entire rooms of furniture, and rather nice furniture at that.

Harry sat down beneath an unfurnished tree and began to sketch the scene. He was still sketching when the man in the bed woke up and saw Harry drawing him.

"Good morning," he called out, throwing back the covers and emerging from the bed fully dressed. "I think I overslept." He got up and stretched and came over to where Harry was sitting.

"What do you do when it rains?" asked Harry.

"I get pretty wet."

"I didn't know people were allowed to camp out in the park."

The man squatted next to Harry. "Oh, they'll probably be forced to move. But until then they pay me to keep an eye on their stuff."

"You mind if I ask a question?" Harry asked.

"Not at all."

"If the people have furniture, and money to pay you, why are they living in the park?"

"Their buildings went co-op and they have no place else to live."

"Are you serious?"

The man nodded. "You tried to find an apartment lately? It's always been difficult, but now it's impossible. All of these people tried, but they couldn't find anything and were finally evicted, so they moved their stuff over here. The trouble is it's going to get cold out pretty soon.''

"Any of them in Kingsley buildings?" asked Harry.

"They're all Kingsley casualties."

Harry wrote down his address on a piece of paper and handed it to the man. "We're having a meeting tonight in order to fight Kingsley. Tell them to send a representative. Maybe we'll be able to help."

"That's like trying to fight city hall."

"Maybe," said Harry, "but people probably said that about the Boston Tea Party."

JAS WAS GLAD she had bought a paperback to read. Harry was home all afternoon, but he must have been working because there wasn't anything to hear. The only break in the monotony occurred every thirty minutes, when he would pick up the phone, dial a number and then hang up. She wondered if he was calling her.

Then, about five-thirty, when Jas was laughing over the unlikely exploits of a Boston-based detective who made Gloria Steinem look like a male chauvinist, Harry's phone rang and Jas put down her book.

"Hello," said Harry after the second ring.

"Harry? This is Blythe."

"Hey, sweetie, how are ya?"

Jas winced at the "sweetie."

"Feeling deprived, Harry. It's been weeks since I've seen you."

"I was in Jamaica, and since then it's been one thing after another. No excuse, though—I should've called."

"I'll forgive you if you'll come by for dinner to-morrow night. We'll have our favorite."

Jas had a feeling it wasn't pizza with anchovies.

"You're on," said Harry. "Shall I bring the wine?"

"Perfect. See you about seven?"

"Can't wait."

Jas was still stewing over this latest development when there was a knock at her door. Thinking it must be Charlie but too paranoid to open it without finding out, she disguised her voice and said through the door, "Who is it?"

"It's me. Arnie."

Jas opened the door and Arnie, two Burger King bags in his arms, slipped inside. "You shouldn't be here," she told him. "Harry would be even more suspicious if he saw you around here."

"I had to see you and you don't have a phone. And I know you won't throw me out because I brought food."

"Arnie, you won't believe everything that's been happening. First of all, Harry knows I was the messenger."

"What'd he say?"

"He didn't say anything to me, but his friend Philly has him convinced I'm some fan of his and I did all of that just to meet him."

"Including pushing Capetto?"

"No, I don't think he has an explanation for that part yet. Then, just a few minutes ago, some woman called him and he's going to her place for dinner to-morrow night."

"Great. I'll bring my TV over and we can watch the game."

"It's not great, Arnie. What's he doing seeing some other woman?"

"You must've left something out, Jas. Correct me if I'm wrong, but you're investigating him at the moment, not dating him, right?"

"He kissed me last night."

Arnie's eyes widened. "Tell me all."

"That is all. But later he told Philly he thought he was falling in love with me."

"Then what're you worried about? She's probably just an old friend of his."

"She sounded sexy."

"Sexy voice, ugly face—it happens all the time."

"Good try, Arnie."

"Well, I'm trying to cheer you up so I can break the bad news."

"What bad news?"

"Maybe I should wait until after we've eaten."

"Arnie, either you tell me now or I throw you out the window to your sudden death."

"Out of the twelve tenants in our building, eight were given eviction notices today. You and I number among the eight."

"Phantom tenants?"

Arnie nodded. "I talked to all of them and we're all in the same boat."

"Those sneaky, rotten bastards."

"Jas, you can hardly talk. How many people did you get evicted?"

"That was my job, Arnie."

"What do you think, some guy investigated us as a hobby? It's not just Kingsley, Jas. Every landlord in the city with co-op intentions is going after phantom tenants."

"I'm going to fight it."

"The only way you can fight it and win is if your aunt rises from the dead. And even if she does, the apartment isn't big enough for both of you."

"What will they do to me, Arnie? Put me in prison for fraud?"

"I don't think they want two hundred and forty thousand more people crowding the prison system."

"I'm going to demand to go to prison."

"I'm telling you, Jas, it isn't that serious. At least, I don't think it is."

"I don't mind. Let the state house us since the city doesn't seem to be able to. At least it would solve my housing problem."

"SO WE'RE ALL GOING to stand firm and not give in to Kingsley's offers?" asked Harry, surveying the tenants crowded into his living room. "Let's see a show of hands."

Every hand in the room went up. "All right, that's what we need," he said, "solidarity. Now, our rent is due on Monday. I say we call a rent strike."

"That's been done before," said 1E, "and they always lose in the end, anyway."

"Yeah, but they've lived rent free for a few months," said 3B.

"There's a difference," said Harry. "Usually a rent strike isn't called until the heat is turned off. We're going to take the offensive in this and call the rent strike first. Furthermore, I was in the park today and saw something interesting. The gentleman by the door, Mr. Voorhman, is going to tell us all about it.''

When Mr. Voorhman had finished telling them about the Kingsley casualties in the park, Harry said, ''They're not the only Kingsley casualties. We're all Kingsley casualties. In this city, right at this moment, there are probably thousands more—some homeless, and some like us, in the process of becoming homeless.''

''What're we going to do about it, Harry?'' asked 6G.

Harry took up copies of future Grogan comic strips he had drawn that afternoon and then had copied. ''This is what we're going to do,'' he said, passing them out.

''THIS IS SO FRUSTRATING,'' said Jas, taking off the headphones and turning to Arnie. ''Just when he got to the good part, he stopped talking. Now everyone's leaving and I still don't know what they're going to do.''

''You mean you're going to tell Kingsley about this?''

''It's my job, Arnie.''

''I sometimes wonder how you can live with yourself, Jas.''

''When you want to be a private investigator you have to take the good with the bad. Don't you remember the night on *Moonlighting* when—''

''Yeah, but that's not real. That's TV.''

''What do you want me to do, Arnie, get a job at Kingsley's selling cosmetics? What's the difference if I'm doing this or defending a criminal? Or not operating on a patient because he doesn't have medical insurance? Every profession has its own guilt trips. At least I'm not an IRS agent—there's your real bad guy. Someday I'll have my own agency and then I can pick and choose my clients. But until then, I do what Stanley tells me.''

TEDDY ENTERED the King's office with trepidation. It always fell to him to bring the bad news to his uncle. ''The legal department has been in touch with me, King, and I think there's something you ought to know.''

''I know nothing about legalities,'' said the King. ''I leave that to the legal beagles.''

''This concerns our new ad campaign, the one about the fat cat.''

King stopped eating long enough to say, ''Yes?''

''Harry Keyes's lawyer has filed for an injunction against the ads citing copyright infringement.''

''Who the hell does he think he is?'' bellowed the King, bits of Danish spraying out of his mouth and garnishing the immediate vicinity.

''Our lawyers say he has a case.''

''Fire them,'' demanded the King.

''Don't you want to hear the good news first?''

''We finally got the bastard?''

''No,'' said Teddy.

''Then it's not good news.''

''Our publicity department did a telephone survey on the new ads.''

''They loved them, right?''

''Wrong.''

''I thought you said it was good news?''

"What I meant, King, was that as long as we're going to be forced to stop them anyway, it's just as well they weren't popular. It would be much worse if we had to stop a successful campaign."

"Give me the figures."

"Eighty percent hated the ad, three percent liked the ad and seventeen percent had no opinion."

"I hate that seventeen percent," said the King. "There's always a percentage of wishy-washy people who can't make up their minds. I'd like to find them and force them to have an opinion."

"Yes, sir," said Teddy, starting to back out of the office. It hadn't been as bad as he had feared.

"Hold it right there," yelled the King.

Teddy held it.

"That detective who's working for us, that Jas Rafferty. What size would you say she was?"

"Rather small," Teddy ventured a guess.

"I meant clothes size, you idiot."

"I don't know anything about women's clothes sizes, sir."

"What I want you do to, Teddy, is go down to our designer department and pick out an assortment of clothes for her. Then find out her address from that idiot who runs Paragon and have them sent to her. I don't like the way she dresses."

Teddy, who had heard stranger requests from the King, didn't blink an eye. "Could you give me some idea what kind of clothes you have in mind, sir?"

"Oh, perhaps a nice robe to eat breakfast in. The kind of clothes women wear to luncheons and teas. A few dinner dresses. And make them appetizing colors, none of those grays or blacks. Maybe cherry red or apricot. Chocolate brown would go well with her eyes. A nice lemon yellow or lime green. Grape. Almond. Strawberry.'' The King's eyes took on a glazed look. ''All this talk is making me hungry. Teddy?''

''Yes, sir.''

''Send along a basket of goodies, too.''

HARRY WAS WORRIED about Jas. He had tried to call her all day yesterday and up until midnight. When he still couldn't reach her today, he decided to drop by her apartment. Maybe she was sick. Maybe she was hurt. Maybe she was ignoring him by not answering her phone, but he didn't really believe that. Everything had been fine when he sent her home in a cab the other night.

When he got to her building and rang her buzzer there was no answer. He noticed that the sign announcing that the building was going co-op was gone, which didn't surprise him. Some New Yorkers would steal anything.

He was about to give up when another tenant entered the building and unlocked the inner door, allowing Harry to sneak in unannounced.

When he got upstairs he saw the eviction notice on Jas's door. He didn't like the looks of that. He hoped she had taken his advice and formed a tenants' association. If she hadn't, he'd come down himself and help them form one. These kind of goings-on in the city were going to have to stop.

He wrote a note asking her to call him and shoved it under her door.

DRESSED IN her brown felt hat and with Charlie's raincoat covering her clothes, Jas followed Harry out of the building. She was justifying this to herself on the grounds that she might find out something incriminating for Kingsley. This didn't really fool her, however. She knew she was doing it because it was better than sitting in an empty apartment wondering what Harry was doing on his date.

Harry headed east and surprised Jas by walking into Central Park. Was he crazy going into the park alone after dark? Was he so naive he thought it was safe in there? He might not know it, but he was damn lucky to have her following him.

No one was going to mess with her, that was for sure. In her raincoat and hat she looked exactly like the kind of person to watch out for in the park after dark. As she followed him down the path, staying a few yards behind him, the few joggers still out gave her a wide berth. Jas smiled when she saw this, as it meant her disguise was a success.

A lot of things about Harry began to annoy her. For one, he was dressed a lot better than she had ever seen him dressed. He was wearing a nice pair of tan pants and a brown tweed sport jacket and his hair looked a lot fuller than it usually did, rather as though he had blown it dry.

Another annoying thing was that his walk appeared jaunty. He looked as though he couldn't wait to get to precious Blythe's apartment. Jas was convinced that anyone with a name like Blythe had to be tall and willowy and blond—Jas's least favorite kind of woman.

What annoyed her out of all proportion was that Harry was whistling. The sound could be clearly heard all the way back where Jas was trailing him, and what he was whistling was "Girls Just Wanna Have Fun." She hoped that wasn't Blythe's theme song.

It was a long walk, clear over to Second Avenue. Jas didn't mind, as the only exercise she was getting in the apartment was when she sat down on the mattress or stood up off the mattress.

When Harry stopped for a moment, Jas ducked into a doorway. When he continued walking, he was holding a bunch of flowers. Jas felt like catching up with him, snatching the flowers out of his hand and shoving them down his throat—in lieu of Blythe's throat, which wasn't handy.

In the next block he turned into a liquor store. Jas, her collar pulled up around her face, watched him through the plate-glass window. He didn't head for the California wines and he walked right past the New York State wines. He seemed to be taking his time making his selection and even asking advice of the sales clerk.

Jas couldn't tell what kind he bought as she was too far away to read the label, but it looked expensive. It looked like the kind of wine that certain people rolled around in their mouths and then made pretentious remarks about. It looked like the kind of wine a yuppie would buy to impress another yuppie.

She was sure it was the kind of wine Grogan would have made fun of, and yet Grogan's creator was now departing the liquor store with the wine under his arm and a smile on his face. Jas was beginning to hope he'd get hit by a taxi. Or, at the very least, mugged. She didn't think she'd even go to his aid.

Jas had been hoping Blythe lived in a brownstone. Brownstones didn't have too many tenants and always had fire escapes, which would have enabled Jas to spy on them. Unfortunately, Harry turned into a large, rather new building complete with a doorman. And the doorman didn't just wave Harry by, either. He made Harry wait by the door while he personally called up to see if he was expected.

That wasn't all bad. At least it meant that Harry wasn't such a regular habitué of the building that the doorman knew him. Unless the doorman was new, which was always a possibility.

Jas hung around the outside of the building ignoring the glances of some of the pedestrians who clearly thought their neighborhood too good for her. One of the people who turned into the building must have reported her presence to the doorman, because he came outside and told her to leave or he'd call the police.

Jas crossed the street and checked out the businesses. There was a nice-looking Italian restaurant whose posted menu didn't look beyond her means. She made sure to take off her coat before she entered, and then requested a table by the window.

While Harry ate his favorite, she'd eat hers. And while he drank his expensive wine, she'd have some house red. But what she'd really like to do was phone in a bomb threat and see the police arrive and clear out Blythe's building. She'd love to see Harry's dinner spoiled as the building was slowly searched.

Harry ought to be glad she wasn't the jealous type or he'd really be in trouble.

AT ELEVEN-THIRTY she was the last customer in the restaurant and the waiters were all standing around the door waiting for her to go home. Jas's temper had reached the boiling point by ten and no amount of wine was able to lower it.

She figured he got to Blythe's place by seven. They'd probably sit around for a half hour and have a drink, do a little talking. Dinner would be served at seven-thirty, eight at the latest. So how long did it take two adults to eat dinner? An hour? Certainly not longer than that. After dinner she was sure there'd be coffee, maybe dessert, most certainly an after-dinner liqueur. And then what? Surely they could have done all the talking they cared to do in that time. So what was keeping him? And if it was what she was thinking it was, then Harry could go straight to hell.

It was even possible that he wasn't going to come out of that building tonight. It was conceivable that Harry and Blythe were going to spend the night to-gether.

She'd give it another hour, but not in the restaurant. She'd wait for him in the park rather than out on the sidewalk. There wouldn't be that many people on the street when he came out and at least she'd be able to sit down. One hour, though; that was it. And if he wasn't out of there by then, she'd go back to his building, break into his apartment, and this time she'd damn sure bug his bedroom.

The lousy sneak!

HARRY'D HAD A GREAT EVENING. He and Blythe went back a long way, a real long way. He had dated her in junior high, Philly had dated her in high school, and the three of them had been best friends ever since.

Blythe, who couldn't even cook as well as Philly, had ordered in from a new Italian restaurant in her neighborhood and the food had been great. They finished off the wine with the dinner while he listened to the troubles she was having with her latest boyfriend.

"Dump him," Harry advised her.

"Harry, do you have any idea what the male situation is in this city? If I dump him, there are two hundred women waiting to take my place."

"You deserve better, Blythe."

"I don't know, Harry. They just don't make guys like you and Philly anymore."

"Philly and I are still single."

"You wanna date, Harry? Or maybe you'd like to fix me up with Philly? Come on, that saying about you can't go home again is true. Anyway, you don't date friends. What about you? Anyone new in your life?"

And Harry, who had a long history of confiding in Blythe, told her about Jas.

"You made that up just to amuse me, didn't you?" she asked him when he had finished.

Harry flashed the boy-scout sign. "Swear to God, sweetie. What do you make of it?"

"That advice you gave to me? I give it back to you double. At the very least she's got problems, Harry. You really need more problems in your life?"

"But she's not boring."

"Oh, no—I wouldn't call her boring. What does Philly think?"

"He thinks she's a Gemini and maybe certifiable."

"Listen to your friends, Harry; that's what friends are for."

When the game started they moved into the living room and Blythe brought out a couple of beers. "I'd like to meet her, Harry."

"You think you can figure her out where Philly and I failed?"

"Maybe."

"I don't know her that well yet. When I get to know her better we'll all get together. She likes the Mets."

"Well, everyone knows Mets fans are crazy. To change the subject, Harry, what's with you and Kingsley?"

It took the entire game to tell her that story.

JAS WAS SHARING a bench with a comatose street person whose raincoat was in better shape than Charlie's. Five minutes before the deadline that she had given Harry was up, there he came down the path, still whistling, still jaunty, a muffler he hadn't been wearing previously wrapped around his neck against the cool night. It was a shocking-pink muffler. Jas felt like strangling him with it.

"Damn," she muttered, moving a little on the bench and disturbing the other occupant, who now appeared to be reviving. Jas sank a few inches into the raincoat so that the lower part of her face was covered.

Just as Harry was neck and neck with their bench, Jas's neighbor to the right called out, "Spare some change for a drink, mister?"

"Shut up," muttered Jas.

Harry ignored the request and was two feet beyond the bench when the man said, "I'm an alcoholic."

Then, just as Jas was preparing to get up to follow Harry, the man beat her to it, staggering after Harry and whining, "It's not my fault; it's a sickness."

Harry was a good two yards ahead of the man when two things happened at once: Harry paused and put his hand in his pocket, and Jas shoved the wino off the path, her hand over his mouth to shut him up.

Harry drew some change out of his pocket and was turning around just as Jas got back on the path. Jas tried every trick she could think of to change the contours of her face, but Harry was already saying, "Jas? Is that you?"

"What're you doing in the park after dark, Harry? Don't you know it's dangerous?"

Harry took a few steps toward her and then stopped. "That was you back there on the bench, wasn't it?"

"I wasn't the one who asked you for money," said Jas.

"I knew it—I knew something was wrong. And then I saw that eviction notice on your door. Is this where you were last night? Sleeping in the park?"

"Harry, I was just taking a walk and—"

He grabbed her and pulled her head into his chest, which effectively drowned out her words. "You're not alone," he told her.

She put her arms around his waist in reply.

"There are homeless people all over the city. It's becoming an epidemic."

She let go of him and ducked under his arms. "Harry, I'm not homeless."

"Don't be too proud to admit it. Just look at you, dressed like that so you'd fit in with the other street people."

Jas looked down at herself. "I rather like this coat, Harry."

Harry grabbed her hand. "Come on, Jas. I'm going to take you home with me and fix you some hot chocolate."

"Quit treating me like a child, Harry."

"Someone's got to take care of you."

She yanked her hand out of his. For all she knew that same hand might have been all over Blythe just minutes before. "I can take care of myself, Harry."

"I know you're proud, Jas, but don't be too proud to let me help you. You'll stay with me tonight."

"With you?" It was impossible to believe that Harry was the type to go from one woman directly to another. And it wasn't all that late—maybe he and Blythe really did spend the evening talking.

"You can have the bed. I'll sleep on the couch."

Jas thought of sleeping in a real bed with real sheets and a real pillow. And Harry in the next room. What the hell, one night wouldn't hurt. And she wouldn't have to sleep with those damn earphones on.

"And I don't want to hear an argument out of you."

Jas grinned up at him. "Who's arguing?"

Chapter Nine

Jas ended up staying through the weekend at Harry's apartment.

"We'll get the *Times* on Saturday night," said Harry, "and first thing Sunday we'll go apartment hunting."

Jas didn't push the issue. If she insisted she wasn't homeless, then how was she going to explain being in the park at that hour? Furthermore, Harry's apartment was a lot cozier than the empty apartment she was supposed to be in.

And apartment hunting wasn't a bad idea. She would be a genuine homeless person pretty quickly.

"Of course, you can also fight it," said Harry, "the way we're doing."

"I'm in there illegally," she told him. "I'm what is called a phantom tenant."

"Maybe there's a way to fight that," said Harry.

Jas shook her head. "No, Harry, there isn't a way."

"If there is, though, I will."

"I know, Harry." Harry was a fighter of lost causes. She knew that already just from reading his comic strip. He saw himself as a kind of urban knight in

shining armor, and right now she was the damsel in the
most distress. She found it touching.

They got into a regular routine around the apartment. Grogan would wake up first and want to be fed,
which would get Harry up. He'd feed the cat and put
on the coffee, the smell of which would awaken Jas.

Harry would scramble eggs while Jas would make
toast; Jas would shower while Harry read the paper;
and Jas would do the dishes while Harry showered.
They didn't get in each other's way as she had thought
two people would do in a one-bedroom, one-
bathroom apartment.

It was cozy living with Harry. It wasn't like real life.
Real life was an alarm clock going off in the morning
and commuting to work and living the exciting and
dangerous life of a private investigator—well, maybe
not as exciting and dangerous as she wanted to believe—and dreaming about the future, when she'd
have her own agency and plenty of money and lots of
men. The time she was spending with Harry was like
a paid vacation.

"There are a lot of jobs in the paper for computer
people," said Harry one morning over breakfast.

Jas had forgotten she was supposed to be unemployed. "I'll check them out," she said.

"You know, Jas, maybe you could do it free-lance."

"Why would I want to do that?"

"I always feel sorry for people who have to go out
to work for a living," said Harry.

"Don't you consider what you do work?"

"Not really. I enjoy it too much for it to seem like
work. And then it's only about an hour or two of actual work every day, which I can do in the comfort of

my own home, and the rest of the time I have to my-self.''

"That sounds pretty boring to me," said Jas, who pictured herself as an adventurer of sorts.

"Lacking the excitement of computers, right?"

Jas refused to go for the bait.

GROGAN WASN'T THRILLED with Jas's presence. After the first night, when he leaped on her bed and then, seeing a stranger was occupying the premises, leaped back off, he had alternately ignored her and made her life difficult.

If Harry and Jas were sitting on the couch, Grogan jumped between them. And stayed there. Whenever Jas opened the front door, Grogan would dart out and she'd have to chase him up and down the stairs. For-merly unadorned sweaters took on the look of angora, and the cat hair caused her to sneeze frequent-ly.

She opened the living-room window wide one morning to let in some fresh air, and Harry, coming into the room, said, "Make that only two inches, Jas. I worry about Grogan getting out on the ledge."

Jas, who had been hoping Grogan would get out on the ledge, reluctantly complied.

"I know what you need," said Harry, and Jas turned toward him in surprise.

"A cat of your own," said Harry. "Right after we find you an apartment, we'll have to go looking for a cat."

Jas had met roaches she was more fond of than Grogan.

HARRY APPEARED TO GET a kick out of dressing her in his clothes. He had insisted on giving her one of his old flannel shirts to sleep in. The first day, when they went for a morning walk in the park, he had handed her a jacket and said, "It's a bit chilly out. Why don't you wear this?" The fact that the sleeves were a foot too long didn't seem to bother him.

In the empty apartment Jas probably would have gone all week in the same clothes, but every morning she would find a clean sweat shirt laid out for her along with enormous socks and a T-shirt. She wore the sweat shirt, went without socks and was glad that he didn't include jockey shorts along with the T-shirt.

She shared his toothbrush, his comb and his nasal spray, something she had never needed before, and had the feeling she was allergic to cats. In many ways she was more intimate with him than she had ever been with any man, and yet, from the time he brought her home that first night, he had not so much as kissed her. She appreciated the fact that there were no strings attached to his offer to stay with him, but she couldn't help wondering if she'd lost her appeal for him.

She took it for two days with the curiosity building up in her, and then she finally asked, "You have something against sex, Harry?"

Harry choked on the spaghetti, spraying tomato sauce clear across the table. "Does this mean we're through discussing politics?"

It did. Jas was bored by politics. "I just wondered, that's all. Going from kissing me to doing nothing just doesn't seem like a natural progression."

"That was different," said Harry.

"I'm afraid the difference doesn't immediately spring to mind."

"You were a single woman in my apartment and I was attracted to you. Under those conditions, anything goes."

"I'm still a single woman in your apartment, so I assume that means you're no longer attracted."

"You're my houseguest, Jas. I wouldn't make a move on a houseguest; that would be taking advantage."

"You're still attracted?"

"Absolutely."

"Well, I'll tell you something, Harry. I'm attracted, too, and I don't have your scruples."

Harry ignored her and started in on politics again.

ON FRIDAY, WHEN HARRY went out to the post office, Jas called Kingsley from Harry's phone.

"It's about time I heard from you," said Kingsley.

"I'm sorry, sir, but the subject seldom goes out and I was afraid to leave in case I missed something. But I've got something for you."

"Let's hear it," said the King, sounding greedy.

"His tenants' association is calling a rent strike."

"He can't do that," yelled the King. "I haven't even had the heat turned off yet."

"There isn't any heat. It hasn't been cold enough."

"The hot water, then. And I'll get the super to make sure the elevators aren't working."

"They don't work now," said Jas. "Anyway, the super's a member of the tenants' association."

"I'll see about that," said the King. "Tell me something, Jas."

"Yes, sir."

"King."

"Yes, King?"

"What're you wearing?"

Jas knew a kinky question when she heard one. "A sweat shirt that says New York Jets. Does that turn you on?" She didn't care if she got fired over that; it was a matter of sexual harassment, as far as she was concerned.

"I didn't know we sold those in Kingsley's."

"I didn't buy it at Kingsley's." And she rather doubted that Harry had.

"Are you a Jets fan?"

"When they win," said Jas.

"You know something, Jas? I have this feeling about you. I'll bet your very favorite dinner is pot roast with sweet potatoes and coleslaw. It's almost like a psychic feeling."

Jas shook her head in disbelief. "That's amazing," she said, "because that happens to be exactly what my mother thinks my favorite meal is. She's wrong, but I don't have the heart to tell her, so she cooks it for me whenever I go home."

"What is your favorite dinner?"

She thought it was a pretty strange question, but she said, "Spaghetti Marinara."

She heard a long, drawn-out sigh. "Well, keep up the good work," said the King. "And please try to get something incriminating on him over the weekend."

Jas thought that was about as likely as finding Mother Teresa was having an affair with the Pope.

HARRY TOOK JAS over to Philly's apartment later that afternoon. Jas ignored the celestial charts on the walls, the crystal ball and other mumbo jumbo scattered around the room and headed straight for the pinball machines.

"Hey, these are great," she told Philly.

"Want to play a game?" asked Harry.

"One minute," said Philly. "There's a price for playing those games."

Jas handed him a quarter.

"Not money. I want to know your birthday."

Jas looked from Philly to the games and back again. "I told you, Philly, I don't believe in that stuff."

"But I do. And they're my games."

"Give it to him," said Harry. "He's not going to be satisfied until you do."

"Please," Philly urged her. "I want to do your chart. I'm curious to know how it looks against Harry's."

"What're you talking about?" asked Jas.

"Charts tell a lot about a person. For instance, name me any great pair of lovers in history and I'll bet their charts lined up."

"What've you been telling him?" Jas asked Harry.

Harry turned slightly red. "All I told him was that I was interested in you."

Jas decided she wanted to play pinball more than she wanted to hold on to her secret. She went over to Philly's desk and wrote down her date and time of birth on a piece of paper, then handed it to him.

"I knew you were a Gemini," said Philly, positively gloating.

"Good guess," muttered Jas.

"It wasn't a guess at all. Astrology is a science."

"So is pinball playing," said Jas, heading in the direction of one of the machines. "Come on, Harry— let's play ball!"

Two hours later Philly interrupted their game by tapping Harry on the shoulder. "Could I see you alone, please, Harry?"

"No, you can't," said Jas. "If you saw something ominous in my chart, I want to know about it."

"Why?" said Philly. "You don't believe in astrology."

"I'm going to be rich and famous, right?"

"I'm not a fortune-teller," said Philly.

"I'm going to die tragically at an early age?"

"I wouldn't consider you to be at an early age."

"Your friend's giving me a hard time," Jas told Harry.

"Come on," said Harry, "let's hear it."

"Well," said Philly, "my advice to both of you is to forget it. In all my years of doing charts, I've never seen a more ill-matched pair. Not only do the two of you have no character traits in common, I think if you lived together for one day you'd be at each other's throats."

Jas exchanged a glance with Harry. "Oh, I don't know about that," she said.

"You needn't think you're putting one over on me," said Philly. "I know you're staying with Harry. What I'm talking about is really living together."

"You tell him everything, don't you?" Jas asked Harry.

"Well, we have one thing in common," Harry told his friend. "Neither of us believes in that stuff."

"Fine, I'm not trying to convert you," said Philly. "Just be warned, that's all."

"Are you warned, Harry?" asked Jas.

"I'm warned. What about you?"

"Oh, yes," said Jas. "Now can we finish our game?"

ON FRIDAY NIGHT Harry invited her along to the fights with Philly, but Jas declined.

"You don't like boxing?" he asked her.

"I eat dinner with my parents on Friday nights."

"You do?"

"Well, sometimes."

"I think that's nice, Jas."

It wasn't nice; it was lying. She loved boxing and she ate dinner with her parents as seldom as possible. Not that she didn't get along with them. It was more that dinner with her parents meant endless questioning from her mother about when she was going to get married and settle down, and equal time from her father about when she was going to get a more adult job.

Instead, as soon as Harry left, Jas took a subway home to get a change of underwear and to see Arnie. When she got there Arnie was sitting on the stoop.

"I'm sure glad to see you," he told her.

She sat down next to him. "What's happening with the eviction?"

"We've got until the end of October to move out."

"It'll go co-op next anyway and there's no way I could afford to buy it."

"So how's it going?"

"I've been living with Harry."

"How big's his apartment?"

"One bedroom."

"I don't blame you," said Arnie. "If I could find a woman with an apartment I'd sure move in with her."

"It's just temporary. He thinks I'm a homeless person and I figured it would be more comfortable than sleeping on Charlie's air mattress."

"An apartment and regular sex; you've really lucked out."

"No sex."

"Then I'm only half-jealous. Listen, you been shopping or something?"

"I've hardly been out of his apartment."

"Well, you had a whole lot of packages delivered. The super's got them."

"I didn't order anything."

"I was here when they were delivered and they had your name right."

"Let's go check it out," said Jas.

Ten minutes later they were in Jas's apartment surrounded by the boxes they'd retrieved from the super. Fifteen minutes after that, Jas said, "Can you believe this stuff, Arnie? Who would wear it?" She was holding up a gold-sequined party dress.

"Get a load of this," said Arnie, pulling a black lace nightgown out of a box. "When did you stop sleeping in T-shirts?"

"This is crazy. There must be thousands of dollars' worth of stuff here."

"And it's all from Kingsley's," said Arnie. "Take a look at the tags."

Jas took a look and shuddered. "So that's why the dirty old man asked me what I was wearing."

"Which dirty old man was that?"

"Kingsley."

"I thought he was some kind of whiz kid. Isn't he only about thirty now?"

"Age has nothing to do with being a dirty old man, Arnie."

"So what're you going to do with all this?"

"I have half a mind to take it all to his office and dump it on his desk. Except there's too much to carry."

"I'll deliver it for you, me and some of the other messengers. No charge."

"Perfect. I'm just sorry I won't be able to see his face."

"You want the cookies returned, too?"

"Everything."

Arnie returned to the box the cookie he was holding. "I don't think cookies are compromising."

"Well, maybe one."

Arnie reached for a cookie. "Or two?"

"Two can't hurt," said Jas, availing herself of the goodies.

HARRY AND JAS went to a movie on Saturday night, then picked up the Sunday paper on the way home. Harry turned out to be serious about checking on the apartment situation. He didn't even read the paper on the couch. Instead, he spread the real-estate section out on his drawing board and had a red marking pen in readiness to start checking off possibilities.

Jas settled on the couch with the sports pages.

After a while Harry said, "I can't believe this. Have you read the real-estate section lately?"

"Not for years," said Jas.

"Me, too. Well, you wouldn't recognize it. Remember how there used to be pages and pages of apartments for rent?"

"I remember."

"Well, now they're all condos or co-ops to buy. There's only a page and a half left of rentals. And very few of those are in Manhattan."

"Read the obituaries," advised Jas. "If they give an address for the deceased, that's usually a good bet."

"How much can you afford?"

"I'm not going over eight hundred."

"I have a feeling that all eight hundred will get you in Manhattan is a share on a studio with two other people. How about Queens? Would you be averse to Queens?"

"I couldn't wait to get out of Queens."

"There's a garage in the Bronx for seven hundred."

"Garage apartment?"

"It just says garage," said Harry.

"Maybe I should share an apartment with Arnie," said Jas. "Together we ought to be able to afford that garage."

Harry looked up. "You and Arnie are just friends, right?"

"Best friends," said Jas. "Like you and Philly."

"Like me and Philly and Blythe. But I don't think I'd share an apartment with Blythe."

"Who's Blythe?" asked Jas, suddenly very interested in the conversation.

"Just someone Philly and I went to school with as kids. We've stayed real close, the three of us. I'd like you to meet her sometime."

"Is she tall and willowy and blond?"

"You know Blythe?"

"I don't think so."

"Well, she's tall and skinny and sort of blond. I haven't seen much of her lately because she's been involved with some guy."

"I'd love to meet her," said Jas.

She was out in the kitchen making them some coffee when Harry yelled out, "I've got it," causing Jas to spill the milk all over Grogan, who reciprocated by biting her leg.

"What was that all about?" asked Jas, going back into the living room.

"Listen to this: 'East Forties, studio with alcove, separate kitchen, six hundred dollars. See super between 4:00 and 6:00.' And it's got the address."

"It's a misprint," said Jas.

"For what? It couldn't possibly be sixteen hundred dollars or six thousand dollars. You've got to be positive, Jas."

"Harry, if there's really an apartment somewhere in the city for only six hundred dollars, people will be killing for it."

"I know New Yorkers have a reputation for violence, but—"

"Harry, I'd kill for it."

"It's only an apartment, Jas."

"No, Harry, it's not. It's the difference between living indoors or living outdoors."

"I think we ought to get there maybe an hour early tomorrow in case other people decide to look at it."

Jas shook her head in wonder. "Harry, have you ever looked for an apartment in the city?"

"I had a realtor find me this one."

"Even at this moment, Harry, there is probably a line forming in the East Forties."

"I think you're exaggerating, Jas."

"Right now as we speak there is someone trying to break into the building and bribe the super."

"I know you have reason to be a little paranoid—"

"I'm not paranoid, Harry. Paranoia would be believing that some idiot put that ad in the paper as a joke. Paranoia would be believing that the address in the East Forties is actually a discount shoe store trying to drum up some business."

"I'll bet you never believed in Santa Claus as a child, either."

"You're damn right, because I'm not gullible."

"Are you saying I'm gullible?"

"If the shoe fits. The discount shoe."

"You want to put your money where your mouth is?"

"Let's hear it."

"We'll go over there now. If there are any people trying to get in to see the apartment, I'll buy you a steak dinner. If there aren't, you'll buy me one."

"Unemployed and homeless as I am, Harry, the prospect of having to spring for a couple of steak dinners doesn't even worry me. Because I'll win."

"You're on," said Harry.

AS THEY APPROACHED Forty-fourth and Second, Harry looked at the line of people and said, "They must be waiting for the late show. I didn't know there was a movie theater around here."

"There isn't," said Jas. "The only late show is seeing who gets the apartment."

"I think you're wrong," Harry said, stopping by one of the couples in line and asking, "Is this the ticket holders' line?"

"I thought we were in line for an apartment," said the man. "Are we in the wrong line?"

"You mean you're going to wait all night just to see an apartment?"

"We've waited longer than that," he was told.

"You believe me now, Harry?" Jas asked.

"This is terrible."

"Just life in the big city."

Harry grabbed her hand and started walking parallel to the line. Some people had brought chairs to sit in, some of them sleeping bags. There were picnic baskets and lots of thermos bottles, and one man, with a crowd around him, had a battery-operated TV set.

"When do you want the steak dinner?" asked Harry.

"Tomorrow night will be fine."

"So, do you want to get in line or what? Make up your mind because it's getting longer by the second."

"You've got to be kidding."

"I waited in line all night once for tickets to the World Series."

"I waited in line all night once for tickets to a Rolling Stones concert, but I was a kid then."

"Well, if you were willing to sleep in the park, I don't see why you're not willing to sleep here."

"Harry, I wouldn't even end up with the apartment. There's a couple of thousand people ahead of me."

"I'd like to stay and see this apartment, maybe talk to some of the people and see if they're being forced out because their buildings are going co-op."

"Harry the crusader."

"It'd make a good strip. You can go on back if you want, Jas. I'll hold your place and you can meet me here tomorrow."

Jas briefly considered it. But she couldn't let Harry sit out all night alone while she was occupying his warm bed. "Let's find the end of the line, Harry, before it gets any longer."

JAS WOKE UP to the sound of music and tried to roll over. The bed felt like a cement wall. She opened her eyes and saw that it was a cement wall and that she and Harry had fallen asleep sitting up against it.

Harry's arm around her tightened as he pulled her back to face him. "The music wake you up?"

She nodded, looking around. Down the block from where they were sitting was a gigantic cassette player and three break dancers. Closer to them was a juggler and to their left a mime. Street vendors were out in force selling everything from fake Gucci handbags to hot dogs with sauerkraut.

"What is this, a street fair?" Jas asked.

"It sure looks like it," said Harry.

The woman in front of them in line said, "They always come out to these things. Apartments get better crowds than street fairs these days."

Jas stood up, her muscles stiff. "I'm going to find a restaurant with a bathroom, Harry. You want me to bring you some coffee and a donut?"

"Sounds better than a hot dog," said Harry.

Jas walked over to First Avenue, finally passing the actual building where the apartment was available. It looked like a perfectly ordinary building to be holding such a gem.

On her way back, there was a man standing out in front of the apartment building making an announcement. Jas stopped to hear it.

"There's been a mistake," he was telling the crowd. "The paper printed the price wrong—it's sixteen hundred, not six hundred." No one in the crowd left.

Jas said to one of the women in line, "You'd pay that much for a studio?"

"It's still not a bad price," said the woman.

A man shouted out to the super, "I'll give you fifty dollars if I can see it now."

"A hundred," another man raised him.

It was up to nine hundred by the time Jas made her way back to Harry. "Did you hear the news?" she asked him.

"Yeah, but I don't see anyone leaving."

"I'm leaving," said Jas. "There's no way I can afford that kind of rent."

"After staying up all night, I'd at least like to see it."

"Are you always this stubborn, Harry?"

"Always."

AT TEN O'CLOCK that night it was their turn to see the apartment. The sleeping alcove had room for a cot, the separate kitchen was in a closet, the bathtub was pint-sized, the only window looked out on an airshaft, and there were mouse droppings in every corner. Jas thought it had possibilities.

The super looked exhausted. He handed Jas an application to fill out and mail in and said, "They'll be processed in order."

"What number am I?" asked Jas.

"I stopped counting when I reached two thousand."

Jas turned to Harry. "That steak dinner I'm getting better be damned good."

"If we can find a restaurant that's still serving at this hour."

"I don't want to hear that, Harry."

"Nothing ventured, nothing gained."

"If I hear one more cliché out of you, Harry—"

"How about, to the victor goes the spoils?"

"I'll show you spoils, Harry, if I don't get that steak dinner. Fast."

"You two are holding up the line," said the super. "What do you think I have, all night?"

THE STEAK WAS thick and rare and succulent. Jas could feel her salivary glands warming up as Harry fooled around with ordering wine, tasting it and commenting on it. She finally said, "Harry, can't we just eat?"

Harry looked chagrined. "I was trying to impress you. Actually, I know about as much about wine as I do about computers."

Jas couldn't help smiling at him. He seemed incapable of lying, something new in her experience of men. She cut a piece of steak and sank her fork into it. "That's more than I know," she said, "but I know a lot about steak. And this one," she added, popping the piece into her mouth, "is fantastic."

Harry was still intent on the wine. "I thought we'd drink a toast."

Jas looked up at him with her mouth full. "Now?" she managed to say without parting her lips.

Harry, appearing to think better of the idea, put the glass of wine down and picked up his own knife and fork. "I don't know how you can eat it that rare," he commented.

Jas, who could've eaten it raw at that point, refrained from commenting.

Jas was already halfway done with her steak when Harry said, "You know, you're cute when you're eating."

"Cute?" The sarcastic tone she meant to give the word was neutralized by her mouth's being full.

"Well, maybe not cute, exactly. More like sexy."

Jas swallowed a less-than-well-chewed piece of meat whole. For a split second it seemed to stick in her throat before continuing its journey. "You've seen me eat before, Harry, and it's never seemed to turn you on."

"I've never seen you eat steak before."

Jas began cutting off another piece. "Are you saying that I eat steak differently from other food?"

Harry nodded. "Other food you just eat, but you seem to be devouring that steak. There's rather an animalistic quality to it that I find sexy."

"You mean like Grogan scarfing down his cat food?"

Harry started to smile. "Kind of."

"Your cat turns you on?"

"No," said Harry, the smile fading. "I have a feeling I'm not explaining myself very well."

"You're not eating very much, either. You want the rest of that steak?"

Harry picked up his steak with his fork and placed it neatly on her plate.

It wasn't rare, but it still looked good to Jas. "You sure you don't want it?" she asked him.

"I'd rather watch you eat it."

"And get turned on."

"All right, so I'm weird. Maybe it's not the way you eat the steak; maybe it's just you. Maybe it's a lack of sleep and waiting in line all day and living with you but not really living with you."

Jas was glad he wasn't asking questions so that she could concentrate on her food.

"Maybe it's the crazy way we met and the way your hair hangs over your eyebrows and how small you look in my clothes and how your eyes get about ten degrees darker when you get mad and—"

Jas paused in midbite to see if he was finished.

"Maybe it's the way you slept with your head on my shoulder all night and the way you made friends with the other people in line and how you never know when to keep your mouth shut and how you pretend to like Grogan when I know you can't stand him—"

Jas stopped eating. "Harry, it's all right—you don't have to explain. You turn me on, too."

"When I'm eating?"

"Well, no, not particularly when you're eating."

"When?"

"Just in general."

"Not at any specific moment?"

"Harry, look, there's a time to eat and a time to be turned on. You understand what I'm saying?"

"This is the time to eat?"

Jas nodded. Except with all the talking about it, now *she* was getting turned on. Which wouldn't do at all. But tomorrow she'd get back to normal living, which meant not staying with Harry, and maybe then they could finally get around to things like being turned on and, further, being able to do something about it without Harry's misguided chivalry getting in the way.

In the meantime, though, a great steak was a pretty good substitute.

Chapter Ten

In Monday's comic strip a homeless Grogan was seen wandering the streets. Everywhere he went he found other homeless cats in alleyways and doorways. Are you a Kingsley Casualty, too? he asked them and they would always reply yes.

Jas got up before Harry that morning and left him a thank-you note on the kitchen table, adding that she was going out to Queens to stay with her parents for a few days. It was time to seriously get back on the job, and that meant no hanging out with Harry.

She was letting herself into the stakeout apartment when a voice behind her said, "What do you think you're doing, miss?"

Jas jumped at the sound of the voice. Trying to act casual, she turned around and said, "Are you speaking to me?"

"I asked what you were doing. As far as I know, that apartment's empty."

"It's not any longer," said Jas.

The man, short and dark with lots of muscles, said, "I'm the super here, and I ought to know."

"I moved in last week," said Jas. "You can check it out with the Kingsley Corporation. They're letting me use the apartment until it goes co-op, at which point I'll be purchasing it."

He still looked suspicious. "Nobody told me about that."

Jas gave him a cool smile. "Why don't you call them and set your mind at ease?"

He seemed to back down a little. "I'll do that."

Jas turned the key and pushed open the door, trying to shield the view of the apartment from the super. She didn't succeed.

"No furniture?" he asked her, the suspicion back in his voice.

"It's being delivered on Friday."

He hesitated for a moment, then said, "I'm going downstairs and will call them. And if you don't check out, miss, I suggest you be out of here by the time I get back."

"I'll check out," said Jas right before slamming the door in his face.

Later, when she reported in to Kingsley, she told him about the super's seeing her.

"Don't worry about it," she was told. "We covered for you. Plus, he's going to be taken care of."

Jas didn't like the sound of that. That's what gangsters always said in movies when what they really meant was that the person in question was soon going to be found floating in the East River.

"How're you going to take care of him?" Jas asked.

"Everyone has his price," said Kingsley.

Thankfully, he didn't mention the clothes being returned. She had been afraid he'd give her an argument about that.

"Oh, Jas, one thing before you hang up."

"Yes, King?"

"There's something I wanted to ask your advice on. It's about my nephew, Teddy. He has this peculiar habit and I was wondering what you thought of it."

"What's that?" she asked.

"He keeps clothes in his oven."

Jas almost dropped the phone. How could it be that Teddy had the same habit she had? Although it wasn't exactly habit; it was more necessity. She had virtually no storage space in her apartment and never used her oven. It had seemed like a reasonable arrangement.

"I wouldn't worry about it," she told him. "He probably just likes his clothes warm."

"Ah. Of course. Yes, that's reassuring to hear. Thank you, Jas."

THAT NIGHT a radio talk-show host asked if there were any Kingsley Casualties out in the radio audience, and more people called in than had called since the night when the radio station had been offering free Super Bowl tickets to the first ten callers.

ON TUESDAY MORNING Grogan was seen talking to a small group of cats. All of them were wearing buttons saying I'm a Kingsley Casualty. What we need is solidarity, Grogan was telling them. All over the city there are thousands of cats, just like us, who are homeless because of Kingsley. In the last square Grogan was saying, "This is what we're going to do," thus leaving all the readers on the edges of their seats, or at least that had been Harry's intention.

Harry's agent called him and asked him if he'd be willing to be interviewed on the five-o'clock news.

"Is this about Kingsley?" Harry asked him.

"They're interested in the Kingsley Casualty angle," said his agent.

"Yeah, I'll appear," said Harry. "And if you can drum up any other personal appearances for me, I'm game."

"I thought you hated that kind of thing."

"Not on this issue," said Harry. "On this I'll take all the publicity I can get."

WHEN JAS CALLED IN on Tuesday, Teddy told her that the King wanted to see her personally and that four o'clock would be a good time.

"Do you know what it's about?" asked Jas, hoping it was going to mean the surveillance was over.

"He wasn't too pleased you returned his gifts."

Jas sighed. "Teddy, if it's about that, I'm not coming in. That has nothing whatsoever to do with business."

"It's not about that; I just thought I'd warn you, that's all."

THE KING WASN'T HAVING a good day. An unprecedented number of employees had called in sick and, when asked the nature of their illness, had said they were Kingsley casualties. Kingsley Airlines reported that ticket cancellations were coming in fast and furious. The lowest blow came when his previously loyal secretary quit.

"I never realized it before," she told him, "but you're the reason I'm back living with my mother in Brooklyn."

"You can't let sentiment interfere with progress," the King told her. "My own brother had to move when I bought up his building and he couldn't come up with the down payment."

"You're heartless," she accused him.

"But very rich," countered the King.

King had other problems that day. At lunchtime there was picketing outside the Kingsley building, the picket signs reading *I'm a Kingsley Casualty.* Kingsley employees caught picketing were summarily fired.

Kingsley queried his legal department on the feasibility of requiring his employees to sign loyalty oaths. The attorney he spoke to told him that only the government could legally require that loyalty oaths be signed. The King questioned the attorney's loyalty. The attorney quit, and King, not wanting to further deplete his legal department, let the matter drop for the moment.

At three-thirty the King had an appointment with Mr. Ruiz, the super in his latest acquisition, the building in which Harry Keyes lived. The King liked all the bases covered.

"It was good of you to come and see me," said the King when Teddy showed the man in.

"Yeah, well, I guess I work for you now," muttered Mr. Ruiz.

"Please have a seat. Would you care for coffee?"

Mr. Ruiz sat down but said no to the coffee.

"Are you happy with your job?" asked the King, his voice oozing friendliness.

"Yeah, it's okay."

"Oh, I'm so pleased to hear that. And your apartment, is that all right?"

"I like my apartment," Mr. Ruiz admitted.

"Wonderful, wonderful," said the King, his round face beaming. Then, quick as a flash, the beam was gone and a stony countenance had taken its place. "Then why, Mr. Ruiz, are you a member of the building's recently formed tenants' association?"

Mr. Ruiz's Adam's apple went flip-flop. "Well, you know, I stand to lose my apartment, too, plus my job."

"You certainly do if you keep this up."

"I do, anyway. I mean, if it's going co-op, there won't be a place for me."

"Not necessarily, Mr. Ruiz. In fact, with your cooperation, you might end up not only with your own co-op but as manager of the building."

"And if I don't cooperate?"

"Oh, Mr. Ruiz, I really don't relish being the bearer of bad news."

"Is that some kind of veiled threat?"

"I trust not overly veiled."

"Listen, Mr. Kingsley, you can't push me around. I was a United States Marine."

"Oh, my, how impressive," said the King, trying not to shake with laughter.

"I was in intelligence."

"I could tell that just by talking to you."

Mr. Ruiz looked slightly mollified. "What would you want me to do?"

"Oh, not very much, Mr. Ruiz. Certainly nothing past the capabilities of a super. For starters, I want the water in the building turned off."

"Is that all?"

"Not quite," said the King. "I believe you have a tenant in your building by the name of Harry Keyes?"

"Yeah, Harry's in the building."

"I want his door removed and the space walled up."

"You can't do that, Mr. Kingsley. That's illegal."

"Not at all," said the King. "It's more in the nature of improvements to the building."

Mr. Ruiz stood up. "I want to thank you, Mr. Kingsley, for the offer of the job and the co-op, both of which you can royally shove!"

JAS WAS WAITING outside Kingsley's office when the super from Harry's building came out the door of the office and she could hear a roar of rage from inside. The super saw her sitting there and his satisfied smile faded. He paused, as though to say something to her, but instead went down the hall in the direction of the elevator.

Teddy poked his head out of the office and said to Jas, "It's your turn," then added sotto voce, "Don't be difficult, now. He's had a bad day."

Jas wasn't pleased to see the boxes she had returned to Kingsley piled up in one corner of his office. She took a seat and said, "You wanted to see me?"

"I'll hear your report first," said the King.

Jas shrugged. "There's nothing to report. From what I've observed so far, the man does nothing either illegal or embarrassing."

"Unlike you," said Kingsley.

Jas blanched, wondering how he had found out she was a phantom tenant.

"You embarrassed me," said the King, "when you returned my gifts."

"Oh, that," said Jas, recovering. "I don't accept gifts from men."

"They were in the nature of a bonus," said the King.

"I'd prefer cash."

"How much?"

"Whatever Stanley deems suitable," said Jas. "Any bonus would have to go to the agency."

The King jutted out his fat lower lip, which made him look very much like a baby who needed a shave. "What if I were to offer you a ranch-dyed mink?"

"Fur makes me sneeze," said Jas, wondering what kind of game he was playing.

"Diamond earrings?"

"Diamonds look tacky with running shoes."

"What about your own co-op?"

Jas stopped breathing at the sound of the magic word.

King gave her a coy smile. "There are a lot of people in this city who would jump at the chance of getting their own legal apartment."

She knew two—herself and Arnie.

"As a bonus?" asked Jas, still not taking him seriously.

"If that's what you want to call it."

"I don't believe you."

"Would you accept it?"

The way things were going, Jas would've sold her soul for a co-op. But not to King. She would trust the devil farther than she would trust him.

"And what would I have to do in return?"

Kingsley smiled. "It's time, I think, to get something incriminating on Keyes."

"I told you, there isn't anything."

"Then you'll plant something."

"Like what?"

"Drugs, stolen goods . . . You're the detective; you think of something."

"Investigator," said Jas, correcting him. She stood up and looked down at him as he sat behind the desk. "I'm not one of your toadies, or lackeys, or whatever you call them," she told him. "I'm a licensed private investigator and my job does not require that I plant incriminating evidence on innocent people."

She could've sworn she heard the King say, "I like her style," as she swung out of his office.

HARRY STOPPED BY the Nouveau Novelty Company on the way to the television studio. They had rushed the order for him and had the buttons ready. In gold letters on a purple background, the button said I'm a Kingsley Casualty. Harry thought the colors were a nice touch: purple and gold were the Kingsley colors.

"I'm a Kingsley Casualty myself," said the salesman. "You mind if I have one of those?"

"Not at all," said Harry, pushing about a dozen of them across the counter.

Then Harry pinned one on the lapel of his sport jacket. He thought it would show up very well on television.

JAS STORMED INTO Paragon Investigations, sailed past Marlene and practically flew into Stanley's office. Only the sight of Stanley outfitted by Banana Republic drew her up short. Up until now Stanley had always favored three-piece suits. Now he looked ready for darkest Africa.

"How's it going, Jas?" he asked her.

Jas drew her eyes away from the khaki vest with seventeen visible pockets and up to where a bush hat partially obscured his recently acquired hair. "I was just with Kingsley," she told him.

"What's the problem?"

Jas sat down and took a deep breath. "Stanley, the man's impossible."

"I don't want to hear that, Jas."

"It was bad enough sitting in that empty apartment night and day," said Jas, feeling justified in lying since she'd still had Harry in her sight. "But now. You know what he wants me to do now?"

"Surely nothing worse than what you did to Capetto."

"How did you find out about that?"

"He complained to the insurance company."

"Does that hurt their case?"

"Don't worry about it—with those dynamite pictures you took, they'll win."

"Kingsley wants me to plant incriminating evidence on Harry Keyes."

Harry spread out khaki arms. "What's the problem?"

"He's a fat, smug, self-satisfied, greedy—"

"Then you should enjoy it."

"I'm talking about Kingsley!"

"And rich, Jas—you left out rich. Do you know what his business could mean to this agency?"

"I'm not doing it. Get Charlie or one of the others to do it, but I refuse."

"It's your case, Jas."

"Sorry, Stanley, but you're going to have to replace me."

"I suppose you know you're developing a bad attitude. Don't you like your job?"

"Yes, I like my job. I also like Harry Keyes. You do it if you have to, and I won't tell Harry, but I'm not going to be the one to do it."

"Kingsley called me and said you were a little upset when you left his office. The thing is, Jas, he wants you. He likes your style."

"And if I won't?"

"Good luck job hunting."

Jas stood up. "You don't have to fire me; I quit."

Which she thought was a great exit line, but Stanley spoiled it by saying, "Just one thing, Jas, before you quit."

She gave him a dubious look.

"Get the equipment back out of that apartment. The other investigators are all out and I don't want valuable equipment like that left in an empty apartment all night."

"You'll have it in the morning."

"See that I do."

HARRY FELT A LITTLE SILLY as he was seated in the chair across from the interviewer and the microphone was adjusted to his pocket. He hated the idea of being in the limelight. It distressed him that after this interview he would no longer be an anonymous face among the millions of anonymous faces in the city. For just a second he found himself wishing that he'd just gone with the flow and purchased his apartment when the time came and not tried to stir up a fuss.

And then the female interviewer leaned toward him and whispered, "I'm a Kingsley Casualty, too; that's why I asked for you on the show," and suddenly he felt a lot better about it all as he remembered how many people could be helped if his crusade gathered momentum.

Another member of the news team finished up a movie review, and then Harry's interviewer was introducing him by saying, "We have with us tonight the creator of that wonderful comic strip, Grogan, which is a favorite of mine and, I'm sure, of our viewing audience. Grogan appears to be embarked upon an anti-Kingsley campaign, and we asked Mr. Keyes to come on the show and tell us about it. So tell us, sir, if you will, what precipitated this campaign."

"Have you been to the Upper West Side lately?" he asked her.

"Not since my building went co-op and I had to move," she said.

"It's turning into Kingsleyland, and in the process, a lot of the most interesting, creative, talented people in the city are being forced to move out. The city's greatest natural resource is being sacrificed to the greed of a few individuals who want to turn Manhattan into one large Co-op City."

"Are you speaking of yourself when you talk about creative, talented people, Mr. Keyes?"

"No, I'm not. And this isn't really a personal ax I have to grind, as I could afford to buy my apartment. I'm referring to all the actors and dancers and musicians that have always been a part of my area of the city. Just as the artists were forced out of SoHo, so are these talented young people being forced out of the Upper West Side. And because it's happening all over the city, there's no place for them to go. But it's all kinds of other people, too, people who have grown up there and lived there all their lives."

"So what can one person do about it, Mr. Keyes, even with the help of such a formidable ally as Grogan?"

"I can't do anything alone," said Harry. "But there are hundreds of thousands of us out there, and if we could join together, I think we'd have the power to stop it."

"How would you do that?"

"I've been told you can't fight city hall, but I don't think that's true. The city is giving permits for these buildings to go co-op, and yet I think we would have the voting strength to put in a new city government, one that would put a halt to it."

"You're going after the mayor as well as Kingsley?"

"I'm going to go after everyone responsible. Someone, at some point, has to say no to this."

"You were telling me before the show about a rally you were planning?"

Harry nodded. "I hope everyone who's watching will spread the word. We're going to hold a Kingsley Casualty rally by the lake in Central Park on Friday night at eight. We wouldn't mind some TV coverage, also.''

"That was Harry Keyes," said the interviewer, "the creator of Grogan. Thank you for coming, Mr. Keyes."

"Thank you," said Harry.

JAS AND ARNIE were sitting in the balcony of a movie theater on Forty-second Street watching a kung-fu movie and eating popcorn. They had seen the movie several times before so it wasn't absolutely necessary to concentrate fully on it except for the fight scenes, which were the really important parts, anyway.

"I'm homeless and unemployed, Arnie. What am I going to do?"

"You're not homeless, yet."

"I had to quit, didn't I? Wouldn't you have done the same?"

"I don't think you want to hear the answer to that, Jas."

"You mean you don't agree with me?"

Arnie's hand snaked into the popcorn box. "You say Kingsley offered you your own co-op?"

"That's what he said."

"I would have planted incriminating evidence on my parents to get my own co-op,"

"It was tempting. After all, a man is usually temporary, but a co-op is forever."

"But you resisted."

"It wasn't just because of Harry. I figured there'd be lots of strings attached."

"Right," said Arnie, "like your own charge account at Kingsley's and free air travel around the world."

"He's weird, Arnie; I think he's psychic. He keeps asking me these peculiar questions as though he knows things about me already."

"Get the co-op. Ask for a two-bedroom and I'll rent one from you."

"Sorry, but when it comes right down to it, I couldn't do it to a friend. A stranger, okay, but not someone I like. You wouldn't do it to me, Arnie."

"I hope I'm never given that kind of chance."

"I know you wouldn't. If anything, you're more ethical than I am."

"So now you can go back to Harry and your romance will blossom."

"That's the last thing I'd do. I'm not going to see Harry again until I have a job and a place to live."

"I can't wait to hear your reasoning on this."

"It's a matter of pride, Arnie. I don't want to be desperate; I want to be on equal footing. Would you want a girlfriend who was broke and had nowhere to live?"

"Only if she was Kathleen Turner."

"He's a really together person and so far I've come off as a complete flake. It'll have to wait a while, that's all."

"But you could tell him the truth now, Jas."

"I can't do that, Arnie. If I blew the whistle on Stanley, I'd be blackballed by every agency in the city. Anyway, I'm not a tattletale."

"You sound like a ten-year-old."

"Well, that's the kind of mentality you have to have to be a successful private investigator."

WHEN HARRY GOT HOME from the news show, Joe Ruiz was waiting for him in the lobby.

"I wanted to talk to you, Harry."

"Did you catch the show?"

"What show?"

"I was just on the five-o'clock news."

Joe shook his head. "Sorry, Harry. If I had known I would've watched it. I was called into Kingsley's office this afternoon. He's after your blood."

"It's mutual."

"He tried to bribe me with a co-op."

"Take it, Joe—you'll probably never get another chance."

"I already turned it down. But we've got a problem, Harry."

"He's turning off the water?"

"He can't do that without my help. It's something else, and I'm still not sure of it. But my feeling is he had a spy in the building."

"You mean you think you weren't the only one he tried to bribe?"

"It's a stranger, someone who doesn't belong here. I saw her going into that empty apartment on four, and I didn't think too much of it other than she might be a squatter. But then I saw her in Kingsley's office. I think she's working for him."

"What can she possibly do? Our tenants' association is no secret."

"It's just this feeling I have. What I'd like to do is take a look in that apartment while she's out. But I'd like you with me so that I have a witness in case she claims I stole something.''

"Sure, let's do it," said Harry.

He followed Joe up the stairs and stood by while the super opened the door to the apartment. He followed him inside and his impression was that it was a squatter. But then he got a look past Joe and said, "What's that stuff over there?"

"It looks like Kingsley's bugging one of the apartments.''

"It has to be me, then," said Harry. "I'm the one who's been going after him."

Joe walked over to the equipment and picked something up. "Ever seen one of these?" he asked Harry.

Harry nodded. "That's funny. My cat was playing with one of those the other night. I couldn't figure out what it was."

"It's a bug. The kind where they can hear every breath you take. I think we should take a look at your apartment."

"Want to get something to eat?" asked Arnie.

"I'm full from the popcorn. Anyway, I have to go pick up the equipment so that I can return it to Stanley in the morning."

"I'll help you."

"Come on, let's take a taxi. I can put it on my expense voucher. In fact, we can really live it up and have the taxi wait for us. It'll only take a couple of minutes to get the stuff."

"I guess you might as well go out in style," said Arnie.

THEY FOUND THE BUGS on the phones right off. The one in the freezer compartment took Ruiz a little more time. Harry, meanwhile, was searching the bedroom.

He was feeling guilty as hell. Jas had been there when his apartment was bugged, and the only thing he could be thankful for was that he hadn't compromised her. Still, it didn't seem fair that because of him she might have been incriminated. She was just an innocent bystander. He would have to tell her, though. It wouldn't be fair to keep something like that a secret from her.

"Found anything in here?" asked Ruiz.

"Not yet," said Harry.

"What you need to do," said Ruiz, "is get a professional in to sweep the place for bugs."

"Are there people like that in the yellow pages?"

"I have some connections," said Ruiz. "I'll get one of my friends over here tomorrow. Or we could play it another way. We could go on as we were and try to throw him off by giving him misinformation."

"No," said Harry. "I don't like the idea of someone listening in on me. I'm not going to have much privacy anymore, anyway, but I'd at least like it at home."

"Let's at least give Kingsley a little trouble," said Ruiz. "What do you say we plant them in the furnace room and let that spy of his listen in vain for a while?"

"I like your sense of humor," said Harry.

"I've always admired yours," said Ruiz.

THEY LEFT THE CAB WAITING and got up to the fourth floor unseen. Jas opened the door and let Arnie go in first.

"Not a bad apartment," said Arnie. "I could live in this."

"You should see Harry's."

"Better than this?"

"Twice as big."

Arnie was looking into the kitchen. "Do you think we'll ever live this well, Jas?"

"By the time we ever make enough to afford something like this, Arnie, it'll be worth ten times as much. Quit looking around and help me or that cab driver's going to be up here looking for us."

"I didn't know you had an air mattress."

"That belongs to Charlie, and it's none too comfortable. Try to get the air out of it, will you?"

Jas unplugged the equipment and rolled up the cords. She got it all together in the carton Charlie had brought it in while Arnie jumped on the air mattress to flatten it.

"Hurry up, Arnie. I want to get out of here."

"I've got to get more air out of it or it'll never fit in the taxi."

Jas got on the other end of the mattress and started jumping in counterpoint to Arnie. She was really getting into the rhythm of it when the door opened and Harry and the super walked in.

"Oh, no," murmured Jas, as their jumping came to a halt.

"That's her," said the super.

"Jas?" said Harry, his look not quite believing what he was seeing.

"Hi, Harry," said Arnie.

"I knew she was working for Kingsley," said the super.

Harry looked betrayed. "Is that true, Jas?"

"It's not as bad as it looks," said Arnie, trying to smooth things over.

Jas looked at Harry and knew she was very close to losing something more valuable than a co-op. "Take the stuff down to the taxi, Arnie," said Jas. "I want to speak with Harry."

Arnie started to get hold of the air mattress, but Harry was already turning away. "We have nothing to talk about," he said.

"Please, Harry."

He gave her one last look. "There's nothing you can say I want to hear," he told her. "Just do me a favor, Jas—never let me see you again."

Chapter Eleven

On Wednesday a politicized Grogan was seen urging all the Kingsley Casualties to write their mayor, write their city council and picket the major real-estate developers.

WHEN CHARLIE REPORTED to Kingsley, he was thrown out of the office.

"Get that idiot who runs Paragon on the phone," the King ordered Teddy.

"Good morning," said Stanley upon hearing Kingsley's voice. "What can I do for you?"

"What was the meaning of sending that idiot over here?" yelled the King.

"That was Charlie, my best operative."

"Is that right?"

"Absolutely."

"Then why wasn't he sent to me to begin with?"

There was a period of silence followed by Stanley's saying, "Ms. Rafferty is no longer in our employ."

"You better start explaining that."

A little coughing, a little silence, then, "I understand she insulted you."

"What's being insulted is my intelligence," said Kingsley, "if you think I'm going to believe you fired her for that."

There was the sound of something hitting against the phone.

"If you're about to pull the 'bad-connection' scam, Stanley, forget it," said the King.

A very small voice said, "Jas quit."

"Get her back," said the King.

"She might be too tenderhearted for this kind of work," said Stanley.

"Tenderhearted? You wouldn't say that if you'd heard the way she laid into me."

"Well, all I can tell you is she quit. Charlie, however, will give you his two hundred percent."

"We won't talk percentages," said the King. "We'll talk results. And the result better be that you get Jas back in your employ or I'll take my business to another agency."

"I'll give it my—"

"Just get her!" thundered the King.

GRACIE MANSION, the home of the mayor, was flooded with phone calls. City-council members were harassed on the street. Kingsley, along with other real-estate development companies, found pickets outside his offices at lunchtime.

As the mayor was breezing along First Avenue he greeted a group of what he thought were well-wishers with, "How'm I doin'?" His erstwhile well-wishers jeered him.

HARRY SHOWED UP uncharacteristically drunk at Philly's office at three o'clock in the afternoon. Philly moved his client off the couch, ensconced Harry in the client's place and conducted the remaining minutes of his session in the front hall.

When his client left, Philly offered Harry coffee.

"I don't want to be sober," said Harry.

"Okay, Harry; you give me one good reason why we should get drunk in the afternoon, and I'll join you."

"She betrayed me, Philly."

Philly sat back down behind his desk. He liked to be comfortable when he listened to people's problems. "I assume you're talking about Jas."

"She works for Kingsley."

It was though his worthless crystal ball finally produced a picture. A picture that made sense. "Okay," said Philly. "It's beginning to fall together. Remember when I said that there might be a reasonable explanation—"

"Shut up, Philly," Harry interrupted him. "I don't care if it's reasonable."

"Sure, that's why she was a messenger. That's why she was out on your ledge. Kingsley was trying to get something on you to put a stop to your going after him with Grogan."

"She bugged my apartment, Philly. My phones! She probably overheard every conversation I had with you about her."

"Brilliant! She was probably bugging your apartment, you came home, and she went out the window and hid on the ledge. That's great, Harry; it means she's not suicidal."

"I should've pushed her off."

"You don't mean that."

"How could she do this to me?"

"She's a Gemini. A classic Gemini leading a double life."

"Double-dealing is more like it."

"How did you find out? Did she tell you?"

"The super and I caught her removing the equipment from an empty apartment in the building. And right before that he'd seen her in Kingsley's office."

"How do you see the guy in the wheelchair tying in?" asked Philly.

"I don't know; I guess he was someone else Kingsley's going after."

"Yeah. That fits. So what'd she have to say when you caught her?"

"Nothing."

"Nothing? That doesn't sound like Jas."

"I wouldn't let her. I didn't want to hear excuses, Philly, or maybe gloating."

"Oh, come on, Harry, it probably would've been interesting. I would've loved to have heard what she came up with."

"I fell for a spy."

"You want my advice, Harry?"

"Not particularly."

"Call her, talk to her. She seemed to like you; I don't think it was all business."

Harry sat up on the couch and shot Philly a bleary look. "Are you crazy? And maybe compromise the cause?"

"What cause is that?"

"The Kingsley Casualties. We're gaining force, Philly; we're going to win."

"I don't seem to be following you."

"Didn't you see me on TV last night?"

"You were on television?"

"I went on to publicize the cause. All the Kingsley Casualties are going to band together and put a stop to co-ops in this city."

"You're dreaming."

"We're going to have a rally in the park Friday night."

"Since when did you become political?"

"When my home was threatened."

"Come on, Harry; you could buy your apartment."

"It's the principle, Philly. I'm fighting for a principle."

"Take my advice, Harry, and forget about the 'cause.' Sometimes you're so noble you make me want to puke. Find Jas, talk to her. Don't lose a good woman because of some misplaced pride."

"You don't care about that, Philly. You're just dying to hear her side of the story."

Philly knew there was a lot of truth in that assessment.

JAS PUSHED THE POT ROAST around her plate, waiting for the opportunity to dump some of it in her napkin when her mother wasn't looking.

"Your problem isn't finding an apartment," her mother said for the third time. "Your problem is finding a man."

"You've always got a home with us," said her father.

"This might come as a shock to you, Mother, but I did find a good man. What I need, though, is an apartment."

"And a job," said her father.

"You really found a man, Jas?"

Jas turned to her father. "What I was wondering, Dad, was whether you'd loan me the money to open my own office. What I was thinking was it'd solve both my problems. I'd have my own agency and I could live there, too."

"You're allowed to live in offices?" asked her father.

"No," said Jas, "but detectives in books always do it."

"This isn't a book," her mother reminded her. "This is real life. What does he do for a living?"

"It's academic, Mother, as he isn't speaking to me."

"I'm sure it was your own fault, Jasmine."

"What do you think, Dad?"

"If I wanted to throw away money, Jas, all I'd have to do is dial China and leave the phone off the hook."

"I'll pay the interest on the loan," offered Jas.

Her father shook his head while managing at the same time to look regretful. "If you came to me and said you wanted to open a boutique on Queens Boulevard, maybe we could talk business."

Jas was incredulous. "A boutique? You think I want to spend all day in a small space surrounded by clothes?"

"It's more womanly," said her father.

"Eat your pot roast," said her mother. "I made it especially for you since it's your favorite."

ON TUESDAY, GROGAN CALLED for all Kingsley Casualties to leave their jobs at ten in the morning, go out into the streets, face in the direction of Kingsley Tower and observe a minute of silence. In the last section Grogan was gazing skyward, a rapt expression on his feline features.

JAS WAS SPENDING the day riding around on the handlebars of Arnie's ten-speed. She was too depressed to stay home.

"I'm really depressed, Arnie," she called out for about the tenth time. It was almost immediately followed by Arnie's stopping so close behind a taxi at a red light that Jas got bounced off the handlebars and onto the bumper of the taxi.

"Sorry," said Arnie as Jas climbed back on.

"I said I was depressed, not suicidal."

"I can't see over you. Could you scrunch down a little?"

"I'll tell you if you're going to hit something."

"You didn't tell me that time."

"That's because I was talking."

"Jas, why don't you just call him?"

"Call him? Why should I call him?"

"Maybe to apologize."

"Do you apologize for your job, Arnie? Anyway, I was going to explain, but he wouldn't listen."

"You're going to lose him if you don't do something."

"You think just like a man, Arnie. The way I see it is he's going to lose me if he doesn't do something. I mean, what does he want? I quit my job because of him, didn't I?"

"Yeah, but he doesn't know that."

"What's that got to do with it?"

"Jas, I hate trying to talk to you when you're like this." He pulled up in front of a building on West Thirty-fourth Street and got off the bike. "Watch it for me, okay? And try to do a little constructive thinking while I'm inside."

"I know what you're talking about, Arnie; don't think I don't. You think I'm depressed about Harry, right? Well, you're wrong. There are plenty of men in this city. It's a job and an apartment I'm worried about."

"Then how come when you had a job and an apartment all you did was complain about the lack of men?"

"Because everything was going well, and when everything is going well you have to complain about something or fate will intervene and give you something real to complain about."

"Are you talking about God?"

"No, Arnie, I'm talking about fate. God has other things to worry about."

Right after Arnie disappeared into the building, Jas noticed a lot of people coming out of stores and offices and standing around on the sidewalk. Then she noticed something even more peculiar. They were staring in a northeasterly direction.

She followed their gaze but couldn't see anything in the sky. She was expecting a Goodyear blimp at the very least, but there was nothing.

She left Arnie's bike unprotected for a moment and tapped the shoulder of one of the women. "What's happening?" she asked her.

"Don't you read Grogan?"

"I recently stopped," said Jas.

"Well, he asked us to stare in the direction of Kingsley Tower for a moment of silence. It's a protest."

"That's kind of stupid, isn't it?" asked Jas.

The woman gave her a murderous look. "What are you, one of those people with your own co-op?"

Out of the corner of her eye Jas saw someone fiddling around with Arnie's bike and went back to claim it. By the time Arnie came out, the people were back at their jobs and she told him what had happened.

"Kind of makes you glad you quit your job, doesn't it?" asked Arnie.

"No, it doesn't. I loved my job, Arnie. I miss it. Yesterday I spent a boring day in Queens. Today I'm spending a boring day riding around with you. Where's the excitement in life if you aren't spying on people?"

"If you're finding it so boring, you can take a hike."

"Just until the movies open, Arnie. Then I'm going to catch the new triple-feature Bruce Lee."

"Oh, yeah, that'll solve all your problems. Don't look for a job; don't go apartment hunting. Spend your day running away from life by hiding in a movie theater. That's sick, Jas—that's really sick."

"Want to go with me?"

"You bet!"

STANLEY CALLED A MEETING of all investigators for five o'clock. Stanley was harried. His khaki shirt was hanging out of the back of his khaki pants. His boots, which he had taken off because they were squeezing his feet and then couldn't get back on, were beneath his desk. His aviator glasses were smudged with fingerprints. His hairpiece was awry.

"She has to be someplace," he said, his hands gesturing helplessly. "What about it, Mervyn? Did you try her place?"

"I broke into her apartment, Stan, but it was such a mess I couldn't tell whether she'd been there recently or not. There's an eviction notice on her door."

"Charlie?"

Charlie shook his head. "I staked out Keyes's place, as you suggested, but she never showed."

Stanley raised his eyes to the heavens. "Anyone?"

"Maybe she split," said Jerry. "She's being evicted, she's out of work. In those circumstances I'd think about leaving town."

Stanley leaned against his desk. "It's absolutely crucial that we find her. You're all on overtime as of now. She's got to be somewhere in the city, and if we don't come up with her soon, we lose Kingsley's business."

"Why'd you fire her?" asked Charlie.

"I didn't fire her; she quit."

"Oh, sure," they all said in unison.

"She did, I swear to it. She went soft."

"Jas wouldn't go soft," said Mervyn.

"Jas always hung tough," said Jerry.

"Jas was one of the guys," said Charlie.

"She did go soft," an agitated Stanley said. "I swear it. If you don't believe me I can prove it; I have it all on tape."

There was a moment of shocked silence wherein Stanley was the most shocked of all. He feared he was now about to be lynched by his investigators. For the very first time his heart went out to Richard Nixon.

HARRY WASN'T HAVING a great evening.

He sent out for Chinese food and then couldn't eat it. He turned on the Mets game and after two innings he realized he didn't have a clue what the score was and turned it off. He called Philly, thinking his friend would come over and cheer him up, but he got Philly's obnoxious answering machine. Or at least the message was obnoxious. It went: "Hi, this is Philly. I'm not here right now, but if you'll leave your name, the time you called and your astrological sign, I'll get back to you." Harry had been in a bad mood already. When he heard Philly's message his mood turned even worse and he left a four-letter word in place of his sign.

At ten o'clock he sat down at his drawing board and began to doodle, his doodling taking the form of comic strips. His mother vented her frustrations by rearranging the furniture; his father took out his frustrations by playing handball; Philly used the tarot cards. With Harry, it had always been drawing.

He drew Grogan following the Siamese cat through the park. Grogan looked rather silly with a lovesick expression on his face, but since this was doodling and not for publication, Harry let it go. Grogan hid behind the bush while the Siamese cat attacked a large Persian cat in a wheelchair. The lovesick expression became one of perplexity.

Harry started a new strip with Grogan and the Siamese cat sitting side by side on a couch. They were looking at each other in a friendly way. In the next square Grogan had moved a little closer to the Siamese. In the last frame they were rubbing noses and the dialogue was all purrs.

The next strip had the Siamese in an empty apartment wearing earphones and looking bored. Then conversation began to come out of the earphones and the look of boredom became one of malicious glee. "Got you, Grogan," said the sly-looking Siamese.

Harry had a little trouble drawing a cat that looked like Kingsley. He had seen pictures of him and knew he was young and fat, but every time he tried to draw a young, fat cat, the cat ended up looking cute. He knew there was no way a man like Kingsley could be cute. He finally solved the problem by placing a crown on the cat's head. The final touches were a mouse hanging out of Kingsley's mouth and the Siamese on his lap. In the last frame he had Grogan bursting into Kingsley's office and catching them together.

Grogan looked as miserable as Harry felt.

ON FRIDAY MORNING Teddy entered the King's office and handed him the *Chronicle*. "Did you see this, sir?"

"I don't read that rag," said the King.

"It's the Grogan comic strip. He's announcing a rally in the park tonight for all the Kingsley Casualties."

"Buy the Rolling Stones," ordered the King. "Have them give a free concert in the park tonight. That'll take care of his rally."

"I don't believe they're for sale, sir."

"Plant a report in the papers that there is topless sunbathing going on in the park."

"At night? This time of year?"

"Why are you disagreeing with me, Teddy?"

"Sorry, sir."

"Do you have a better idea?"

Teddy availed himself of a chair and sat down, crossing his legs. It was the most relaxed he had ever appeared in front of Kingsley. "Well, I did have an idea."

"I can't wait to here this," said the King.

Teddy smiled. "What I thought, King, was that we could have calls placed to every satisfied owner of a Kingsley co-op, asking them to go out and protest the rally."

"Your brains have gone soft, Teddy. People aren't going to do that out of the goodness of their hearts."

"I've worked for you long enough to know that, King. What I thought was we could reduce the interest on their mortgages by one percent."

The King bestowed a glowing smile on his nephew. "I'm proud of you, Teddy. You're learning, you really are."

HARRY SPENT THE MORNING getting the necessary permits to hold the rally. He was feeling better about things. It hadn't worked out with Jas, but now he had a real mission in life and he was going to devote all his available time to it. He would be the Joan of Arc of Manhattan, leading all the homeless back to their apartments. No, not Joan of Arc; she was a woman and he wasn't feeling well-disposed toward women. St. Patrick, that's who he'd be. St. Patrick leading all the yuppies into the East River. And it wasn't a bad idea for a Grogan comic strip, either.

THE THREE BRUCE LEE MOVIES of the day before hadn't served to lift Jas's depression. She missed her job. And she knew she was going to miss her apartment soon, too.

Most of all, though, she missed Harry.

If he would only listen to her, she knew she could explain things satisfactorily. She would tell him that she had only been doing her job, that it wasn't anything personal. She would confess that she had been attracted to him at once and that as she grew to know him better, she had started to fall in love with him.

And then he would say, "If you were falling in love with me, how could you spy on me?"

That was kind of a difficult question to answer. That, in fact, might be a good time to throw herself in his arms and rely on chemical reactions.

And if there wasn't a chemical reaction on his part?

Then she would have to rely on her wits. "It's like being a spy," she would tell him. "Sometimes spies have to collaborate with the enemy, but then they find themselves becoming practically involved. But you don't betray your country, Harry."

And Harry would say, "I didn't know Kingsley had bought up the entire country yet."

Even her fantasies were depressing her.

HARRY HAD LUNCH with Philly. "You going to come out and show your support tonight?" he asked his friend.

"My building hasn't gone co-op yet, Harry."

"It will. It's never too soon to protest it."

"I don't get it, Harry. Why don't you put all your energy behind something really important, like saving the whales?"

"I didn't know you liked whales, Philly."

"I don't like whales. I don't dislike them, either; I just don't know any."

"Reason number one, Philly, is that a cat trying to save whales would be a joke. I mean, they're fish, right? And cats eat fish."

"I don't think they're fish exactly."

"Philly, this is immediate. This is now. The yuppies are taking over the city and someone's got to stop them."

"The yuppies? I thought you were going after Kingsley."

"I'm going for it all, Philly."

Philly decided he needed a drink with his lunch. "How about you, Harry?" he asked.

"No. I want all my wits about me for tonight. You'll come out with me, won't you, Philly?"

"Maybe I could tell a few fortunes."

"This is a rally, Philly, not a circus."

"Somehow I'm not altogether convinced of that."

JAS FOUND HERSELF on Harry's block, walking in the direction of Harry's building. She'd ring his buzzer and if he was home, maybe he'd talk to her. She'd rather not be the one to make the first move, but she was pretty sure if she didn't make it nobody would. Harry didn't strike her as the kind of guy who'd say he didn't want to see her if he didn't mean it.

She was the type to say something like that. She, in fact, said things like that to guys all the time, confident that they'd know she didn't really mean it. She always liked to have confirmation that they wanted to see her badly enough to ignore something like that and see her anyway.

She had a feeling Harry was a little more straightforward than that. Which meant that Harry could never in a million years make it as an investigator.

She went into the foyer of his building and pressed his buzzer. She pressed it again. She pressed it for a third time. And then, without even thinking about it, her hand reached in her pocket for a credit card, and before she knew what she was doing, the door to the lobby was open and she was headed inside. It gave her a good feeling, as though she were back on the job again.

She took it at a steady pace up the stairs and knocked at his door. She knocked a second time before picking the lock with the tool she just happened to have in her pocket.

Harry wasn't home; Grogan was. Grogan, who should have known her by now, had the nerve to hiss at her. She had half a mind to open the window and let Grogan loose on the world.

She decided to leave Harry a note. She'd make it a nice note, the kind that might touch his heart. She would tell him she missed him. She would tell him she quit her job because of him. She might even go further and hint that she loved him, if she could figure out how to convey that without actually saying it. Spelling it out would leave herself open and she always avoided things like that.

What she wouldn't do was leave the note in his apartment. She didn't think he would take kindly to her breaking in once again. But she'd use his paper and write a note and then take it downstairs and tape it to his mailbox.

She went over to the drawing table and took a pencil out of the mug. Grogan snarled at her before jumping off the table and onto the floor. She sat down on the stool and went to lift the drawing paper up off the pad to find a clean sheet when she noticed what was on the drawing paper.

She looked at the strips depicting Grogan, the Siamese cat and Kingsley. She was not amused. Nice, straightforward Harry was getting ready to immolate her on the pyre of his comic strip. Harry was out for revenge!

FIVE KINGSLEY CASUALTIES were arrested at three that afternoon for nailing a sign onto Gracie Mansion saying that it was going co-op. The press picked up the story and they were thereafter known as the Gracie Mansion Five.

JAS MARCHED into Paragon Investigations, ignored Marlene and headed straight for Stanley's office. "I want my job back," she announced to him.

Stanley didn't succeed in hiding his elation. "No problem. I haven't even had you taken off the books."

Jas, sensing a victory she hadn't anticipated, said, "And I want a raise, Stanley."

"Would fifty dollars a week be all right?"

She gave him a suspicious look. "Why are you being so nice to me?"

"Kingsley threatened to take away his business if we didn't get you back. He's taken quite a shine to you for some reason."

In her anger, Jas had forgotten about that. "He gives me the creeps, Stanley."

"But you'll work for him?"

"Oh, yes. I very much want to work for him."

"Great. Let me get him on the phone and give him the good news."

THE KING WAS SO HAPPY he sent Teddy out to get him a seven-layer cake. He consumed it while running his latest fantasy about Jas through his head, the one that ended up with "happily ever after."

Chapter Twelve

Jas met with the King at six o'clock. It was a dinner meeting, but Jas wasn't eating.

"You want me to do what?" she asked in astonishment.

"All you have to do, Jas, is organize a counterrally with the yuppies."

Jas looked with loathing at the quantities of food piled up on the table and pushed her chair back. "I don't know how to do that; what you need is a union organizer or someone who knows how to put on rock concerts. Why don't I just spy on the Kingsley Casualties rally?"

"Because it's not secret, that's why. Anyone can spy on it."

"Well, I don't want any part of it. I hate yuppies."

"You're young, aren't you?" asked the King.

"I guess."

"You live in a city."

Jas wondered what the point of this was.

"And aren't you a professional?"

"Of course I'm a professional."

"That makes you a yuppie," said the King.

Momentarily shaken, Jas said, "I'm sure you must be wrong about that. I couldn't possibly be a yuppie. Yuppies can afford to buy co-ops."

The King smiled. "You'll be able to afford a co-op if you stick with me, Jas."

Jas pulled her chair back up to the table and started to fill her plate.

SEVERAL THOUSAND Kingsley Casualties showed up at the park for Harry's rally. They were all ages, members of dozens of different ethnic groups. The site resembled a picnic ground, with people seated on blankets and hampers of food spread out. Scattered around were pictures of Grogan fastened to stakes and stuck in the ground. The odd Mets pennant was also seen. Harry, with a bullhorn, stood on a hastily constructed platform.

The three major television networks were there with cameras, and newspaper reporters were working the crowd, trying to get human-interest stories for their papers. A few politicians, who always came out wherever there was a crowd, were shaking hands and kissing babies and passing out campaign literature.

The mayor stayed home.

"Welcome, Kingsley Casualties," Harry's voice boomed out to the crowd.

A little desultory cheering was heard.

"Some of us have come up with what we believe to be a foolproof plan to foil Kingsley."

There was scattered applause but the majority of hands were busy holding beer cans or hot dogs.

"What we're going to do," yelled Harry, "is take our buildings hostage!"

A lot of blank faces stared up at him.

"Let me explain," said Harry. "Now I know a lot of you have already lost your apartments. Those of you who have will, instead, march en masse to Gracie Mansion and camp out on the front lawn."

"It's cold out tonight," someone yelled from the crowd.

"Tents have been donated by Jordan's Sporting Goods Emporium."

Harry noticed some movement on the edges of the crowd but thought it was more Kingsley Casualties arriving. "The rest of you," he said, "will take your buildings hostage. What we're going to do is barricade the buildings and not allow in building inspectors, workmen or real-estate salesmen. And if your building has an unsympathetic super, one who's siding with Kingsley, throw him out. What we're doing is declaring war on Kingsley."

The cheers were almost rousing.

"Kingsley has power," said Harry, "but might does not make right. We've got right on our side and we're going to give the power back to the people."

A few fists were raised.

Ruiz stepped up on the platform and whispered to Harry, "I don't know whether you've noticed it, but we're being surrounded by yuppies."

Harry looked out at the fringes of the crowd. What looked like an army of safari guides was twelve deep around the Kingsley Casualties. And directing them, with a bullhorn of her own, was Jas.

"We're being infiltrated by Kingsley's people," yelled Harry, causing the crowd to turn their heads for a look. "And that one with the bullhorn, the one with the orange sweat shirt, is Kingsley's personal spy, who only this week had my apartment bugged.''

The Kingsley Casualties began to grumble.

Jas put her own bullhorn into action. "People, don't listen to him. He's a rabble-rouser whose only interest is selling more comic strips.''

One of the Kingsley Casualties yelled, "She's a Grogan hater," and the crowd's grumbling picked up.

"He's asking you to break the law," yelled Jas. "You take those buildings hostage and you'll not only end up without an apartment, you'll end up in jail!''

Jas's group began to do a little tasteful grumbling of its own.

The television cameras were kept busy switching back and forth between the two groups, and the politicians were momentarily at a loss as to which group they should go after. Most of them defected to Jas's crowd under the assumption that people with dwelling places were more likely to register to vote.

Philly, who had been watching the scene with amusement, jumped up on Harry's platform and grabbed the bullhorn out of his hand. "Let me tell you a story of trickery and deceit," he yelled, and the crowd settled down.

"That Kingsley spy in the orange sweat shirt," he said, "did the dastardly deed of moving in with Harry Keyes, whom you all know and love as the creator of Grogan, with the express purpose of spying on him.''

There were a few lewd whistles from the crowd.

"That's a bald-faced lie, Philly," yelled Jas, wishing she had dressed more sedately instead of wearing her orange sweat shirt that almost glowed in the dark.

"She's a Gemini," said Philly, "and we all know how sneaky Geminis are."

"I'm a Gemini," yelled one of the Kingsley Casualties, and others in the crowd nodded.

Harry grabbed the bullhorn away from Philly. "Go tell a few fortunes," he said to his friend.

"I didn't move in with him to spy on him," shouted Jas. "I moved in with him because I liked him."

"If you moved in with me because you liked me, you have a funny way of showing it," shouted Harry. "When you like someone you don't plant bugs in his apartment."

"You don't humiliate her in comic strips, either," Jas cried out.

"Let's get the yuppies," yelled one of the Kingsley Casualties. Others took up the cry.

"Let's remain calm," yelled Harry, but it was already too late. Hundreds of male Kingsley Casualties, beer cans in hand, were standing up and starting to storm toward the yuppies. Hundreds of male yuppies were setting down their wine coolers and raising their fists in classic pugilistic style.

What became known as the Famous Friday Night Fracas was about to begin.

IT WAS A SLOW WEEKEND for news so the media people made the most of the Grogan vs Kingsley affair.

Saturday, which was being called "day two of the hostage situation," found the city jails filled with protesters. A tent city had been erected around Gracie Mansion, precipitating the out-of-town trip the mayor took over the weekend. All over the city, soon-to-be Kingsley Casualties barricaded their buildings while individual tenants leaned out of windows to give interviews to the press. Yuppies, finding their popularity at a low ebb, stuck close to home.

A highly rated Saturday-night television show that was shown live from New York featured several skits dealing with Grogan, yuppies and Kingsley. The skits about the yuppies and Kingsley were not flattering.

Harry spent most of Saturday talking on the telephone with the press. Kingsley held a strategy meeting with Teddy. Jas and Arnie went to Hoboken to look at apartments.

DAY THREE OF THE HOSTAGE SITUATION found most of the people jailed in the fracas out on bail. The inhabitants of the tent city were entertained by a group of visiting gospel singers. Most of the city turned on their television sets and watched the Giants demolish the Cowboys.

Harry began to go stir-crazy and wondered if barricading the buildings had been such a good idea.

Kingsley had a champagne brunch that went on for hours.

Arnie spent the day giving Jas a hard time.

"I thought you were my friend," she told him at one point.

"I'm probably your only friend," said Arnie. "You and your group aren't exactly popular in the city. Did you see where the *Chronicle* is calling you the Gemini Spy?"

"I'm fighting fire with fire, Arnie. I think I'm entitled to do that."

"I can't believe you really think Harry would have gone after you in his comic strip."

"I saw them, Arnie, in black-and-white."

"It's not in his character. From meeting him, and from everything you've told me about him, I don't believe he would've done it."

Somewhere in Jas's subconscious she knew that, just as she also knew her conscious mind was using it against him to justify getting her job back. "You don't know that, Arnie."

"Leading a bunch of yuppies! You're a disgrace to your class, Jas."

"What class is that?"

"Those of us who are being thrown out of apartments. What I should have done was come out there with all two hundred and forty thousand phantom tenants. We're the ones who need some rights."

"We wouldn't have to be phantom tenants anymore in Hoboken."

Arnie buried his head in his arms and groaned.

ON DAY FOUR of the hostage situation, Kingsley called Jas to his office for a breakfast meeting. Jas, who had already had an Egg McMuffin, sat in silence while the King noisily ate.

When he finished licking the last bits of sugar off his lips, King said, "You're going to go in there as our negotiator, Jas."

"Go in where?" she wanted to know.

"Straight to Harry Keyes."

"How do I get to Harry Keyes when his building is barricaded?"

"You're an investigator; you'll think of something."

"What am I negotiating?"

"I've been informed that he's lost us a lot of money, and it's getting worse by the minute. Half my employees are home in barricaded buildings. All over the city my contractors are being refused access to the buildings being renovated. It's beginning to make me lose my appetite, Jas. I'm willing to cut a deal."

Jas would have bet Kingsley would never back down. "What kind of a deal?"

"Offer Keyes his own co-op."

"I don't think that'll do it, King. He could afford to buy it if that's what he wanted."

"Tell him we'll put off going co-op for two years if he'll cease and desist."

"Okay, that gives me something to bargain with, but what's the bottom line?"

"If it comes to that—and I'm relying on you to make sure it doesn't—the building won't go co-op."

"What about the other buildings?"

"Oh, no—I'll give in to Keyes's building because he's becoming a royal pain, but the others will go forward as planned."

"Okay," said Jas, standing up. "That gives me something to work with. I'll get back to you later."

She was walking out of the office when the King called out, "I'm curious about something, Jas."

"What's that?"

"Why are you lousy at math?"

"What?"

"I get the distinct feeling, and don't ask me why I'm getting it, that you flunked algebra."

"I'm not lousy at math. I flunked algebra because I was caught cheating on a test."

He certainly seemed psychic. But if he was really psychic, why hadn't he picked up on her feelings for Harry? She said, "King, what is it with all these questions? All these 'feelings' you're getting about me?"

King's smile was gratified. "Did you ever meet someone, Jas, and think you knew all about that person?"

"No," said Jas.

It was her turn to feel gratified as his look turned to one of chagrin. Maybe now he'd give up on all the personal stuff and just stick to business.

HARRY WAS BORED. He was so bored he was watching a daytime game show designed to drive anyone with a modicum of intelligence up the wall. In theory, barricading the building had sounded exciting and adventurous. In reality, it was like being back in high school and getting grounded by his parents. He saw co-op activism becoming a way of life and didn't like what he saw.

He got up to turn off the TV and heard shouting coming from the street. He wished the TV people and the reporters would go somewhere else and leave him alone. Only the fact that he made his own living from newspapers kept him from refusing to speak to them.

He went over to the window and opened it. He stuck his head out and heard, "Hey, Gemini, you spying for Kingsley again?"

He swiveled his head to the left and saw Jas very carefully making her way along the ledge. His first impulse was to slam the window shut. Then she shouted down to the reporter, "No comment," and Harry had to smile.

He opened the window all the way and climbed out onto the balcony. He crossed his arms and leaned against the balcony, preventing her access. "You going to jump this time?" he asked.

"You wish," muttered Jas, stopping within two feet of him and placing her hands on either side of her against the building.

"You going to invite her in, Harry?" yelled Anderson of the *Chronicle*.

Harry grinned down at him. "Never let it be said that Harry Keyes makes the same mistake twice."

There was laughter from the street.

Jas glared at him. "I wasn't going to jump that time."

"I figured that out. I imagine that's when you bugged my apartment."

"It was not. I was just searching the place that day."

"Lovely," said Harry. "I imagine there are some people who admire that kind of behavior."

"Are you going to let me in?"

"I think not. But if you get bored out there, I'll have Philly come over and read the tarot cards for you."

"How is Philly?"

"Philly's fine. He's not quite clear in his mind about the man in the wheelchair, but he feels most of the mystery about you has been cleared up."

"Hey, Harry," yelled one of the cameramen. "Lean over a little farther so we can get you both in the picture. You're on live, guys."

Harry, instead, backed away a little.

"The man in the wheelchair had nothing to do with you," said Jas.

"We figured that," said Harry. "It just didn't seem to make any sense."

"That was for another client."

"Client? What kind of clients does Kingsley have?"

"I don't work for Kingsley," said Jas.

That was such a patent lie that Harry moved to go back through the window.

"Don't leave, Harry," yelled the reporters.

"I'm telling the truth," yelled Jas.

Harry sat down on the windowsill. "I don't think you'd know the truth if you fell face into it."

Moving very carefully, Jas reached into her back pocket and took out a wallet. She held it out to him. "Take a look at my ID card," she told him.

Wondering what kind of game she was playing, Harry took hold of her wallet and flipped it open. "This says you're a private investigator."

Jas nodded. "I work for Paragon Investigations. Kingsley is one of our clients. I was only doing my job, Harry."

Harry handed the wallet back to her. "You think that excuses you?"

"Yeah, I do. I'm not going to apologize for doing my job. I'm a damn good investigator."

"Oh, yeah, you're great. Don't forget, I caught your shove-the-guy-in-the-wheelchair-in-front-of-a-car act."

"I could explain that, Harry, only it happens to be confidential."

Harry leaned over the balcony. "Hey, did I tell you guys about the time I saw the Gemini Spy shoving this handicapped man—"

"Shut up," yelled Jas. "Okay, I'll tell you. He was claiming to be paralyzed from an accident and we were investigating him for the insurance company involved."

"Lovely line of work you're in," observed Harry.

"I'd say it's a little more stimulating than sitting home and drawing pictures of cats!"

Harry straightened up. "Well, I think I'll go inside and draw some pictures of cats and leave you to be stimulated on the ledge. Take care, now—don't fall off."

He was halfway through the window when she called out, "I'm here to negotiate."

Harry paused. "Why didn't you say so?"

"I'm saying so now. Kingsley sent me over to make a deal with you."

"Then Kingsley's not as intelligent as I've heard he is. Why didn't he send someone I could trust?"

Jas looked as though she wished he were the one on the ledge so that she could shove him off. "He doesn't know about that, about things getting personal with you."

"I'm afraid I don't know about it, either," said Harry.

"You know damn well what I'm talking about," yelled Jas.

"Tell us," shouted one of the reporters.

"So, you're not honest with me and you're not honest with Kingsley. What the hell kind of negotiator does that make you?"

"Damn it, Harry, I quit my job because of you."

"Oh? Why was that? Because you had to lie to me?"

"Not exactly."

"Well, just what exactly was the reason?"

"I was supposed to plant incriminating evidence in your apartment."

Harry, who was beginning to feel as though he was in the middle of a spy book, shook his head in amazement. "I don't get it, Jas. Is there some moral distinction between lying and spying, and planting false evidence?"

"I don't know about moral, but lying and spying were fun. Planting incriminating evidence on you, though, would have been serious business. I didn't want you going to jail."

"This is quite illuminating, Jas. In just a few minutes I've learned more about your character than I did living with you for three days. But to get back to what you said before, if you quit your job because of me, what are you doing here?"

"It's because of those comic strips you drew of me, like the one with me on Kingsley's lap. When I saw those I thought, The hell with you, and got my job back."

"How could you possibly have seen those?"

"I'd rather not tell you."

"I'd be interested to know. To my knowledge they've never left my drawing table."

Jas shifted her footing and gave him a pained look. "Couldn't we discuss this inside?"

"Not yet," said Harry.

"Well, I came over to see you, but you weren't home."

"So, naturally, you broke into my apartment."

"I wanted to leave you a note."

"Other people use the phone."

"I didn't mean to snoop that time, Harry."

"Nor did I mean to publish those strips. It's just my way of working off frustrations."

She gave him a delighted smile.

"What're you smiling about?"

"You were frustrated because of me, Harry?"

"Jas, you've done nothing but frustrate me since the day you appeared on my ledge."

"It was frustrating for me, too, you know. You think I like having to lie about everything?"

"I think you rather enjoy it."

"Harry, I hate computers."

"We're even then. I hate Bruce Lee movies."

Jas seemed to pull away from him.

Harry raised his voice. "That was my only lie, Jas, and I was worried about leaving you alone. I thought you were suicidal, dammit!"

"Get a net, someone—she's suicidal," yelled one of the reporters.

Harry reached out his hand. "Come on inside and we'll negotiate."

The reporters were heard to groan.

Chapter Thirteen

When Grogan spotted Jas coming in the window, he promptly left the room.

Jas was glad to be off the ledge. She didn't admit to being afraid of anything, but standing on a narrow ledge several floors off the ground wasn't one of her favorite things. "Got anything cold to drink?" she asked Harry. Her mouth was dry from breathing in all that fresh air.

"First we negotiate, then we'll celebrate with a drink," said Harry. He sounded more decisive than usual.

Jas collapsed on the couch and put her feet up on the coffee table. "Come on, Harry, I'm dying of thirst. One beer, okay?"

Harry sat down on the stool and rested one elbow on the drawing table. "Let's hear the offer."

Decisive and stubborn. She tried a sweet smile, or at least something that she hoped passed for sweet. "I might be easier to negotiate with if I have a beer to relax me."

"It won't work, Jas. I've had a few beers with you, if you recall, and you're no easier to get along with when you've had a few than when you're dead sober."

Was this a new Harry? A forceful Harry? Somehow she doubted it. "Could you spare a glass of water?"

Harry grinned. It wasn't the usual Harry sort of smile. She supposed it could actually be called cunning. He looked at his watch and said, "You have thirty seconds to make your offer; then it's back on the ledge."

Jas didn't care for intimidation, even from someone as unintimidating as Harry. She slowly got up from the couch and headed for the window. She was very sure that as soon as she began to climb out, Harry would give in and offer her a drink. Harry was too much of a gentleman to force her back onto the ledge.

Jas got to the window and swung one leg over the sill. When Harry didn't say anything, she sat down on the sill and pulled her other leg over. Total silence behind her. She stood up on the balcony and a couple of reporters caught sight of her, so she sat back down out of their view. Still nothing from Harry.

She couldn't believe he was being as stubborn as she was. If they were both going to be stubborn, nothing would get accomplished. And if he expected her to be the one to give in, it was damn sure nothing would get negotiated. Jas didn't believe in giving in. Giving in did not fit her self-image.

She sat there with her back to Harry for what seemed like a very long time. No entreaties from Harry were heard. She began to feel extremely foolish. It had been a bad move. She should've stayed on the couch and begun the negotiations. Now she was going to be forced to give in and that would place her in a weakened bargaining position.

She turned her head to see what Harry was up to. What Harry was up to was enjoying a can of beer. Furious, she swung her legs back over the sill and stood up. He took a long swallow from the can and ignored her.

Jas decided to pretend she wasn't thirsty and also to pretend he wasn't drinking a beer. She sauntered back to the couch and sat down, her feet again going to rest on the coffee table. "Okay," she said. "Here's the offer. Kingsley's willing to allow you to remain here indefinitely as a renter if you drop your vendetta against him."

Harry set down his can of beer and began doodling on a sheet of drawing paper. He could have been alone in the room for all the attention he paid to her announcement.

Jas saw Grogan emerge from the bedroom and sit in the hall, glaring at her. "Well, that's what you wanted, isn't it? Your apartment won't go co-op."

Harry looked up from his drawing and gave her a quizzical smile, as though just noticing she was in the room with him.

"Will you say something, Harry?"

"You want to use my phone?"

"No, I don't want to use your phone."

"I just thought you might like to call Kingsley and tell him you struck out."

Harry went back to doodling, Grogan was now washing the regions in the vicinity of his tail, and Jas was now not only thirsty but frustrated. "You're turning down an offer I'd die for," she told him.

He gave her an interested look. "Are you that easily bought off?"

"We're talking apartments, Harry. We're talking the difference between living indoors and living on the street."

Harry took another long swallow of beer, then gave a little sigh of satisfaction. It was so perfect it could have been a beer commercial.

"All right, listen. I would like to use your phone. But I'd like some privacy."

"You can use the one in the bedroom," said Harry.

When Grogan saw her coming down the hall toward him, he raced past her into the living room as though she were out to attack him. She closed the bedroom door and used the phone to order a pizza and a six-pack of beer.

When she got back to the living room, she settled herself on the couch again before saying, "I understand you feel some responsibility to your tenants' association, so how about a two year extension before Kingsley turns your building co-op?"

"Fine. Come back and talk to me in two years."

"Harry, the other tenants will be delighted. You'll have won."

"I don't know why I should have to explain the obvious to you, Jas, but no one is going to want to move in two years any more than they want to move now. And you, of all people, should know the apartment situation. And speaking of apartment situations, where are you living these days?"

Jas avoided his eyes. "My building isn't exactly going co-op."

Harry shook his head. "I wonder why I don't find that surprising."

"I'm in just as bad a position, though. I'm a phantom tenant."

"Do you do anything legally?"

"We can't all be saints, Harry."

He gave her a surprised look. "Is that what you think?"

"All I can say, Harry, is that if you were that much of a goody-goody as a child, I probably would've punched you out."

"What were you, the neighborhood delinquent?"

"I was human, okay?"

Harry turned back to his drawing, saying, "Come over here a minute, Jas."

He seemed intent on his drawing and she figured he was writing out his own terms of negotiation. She got up and walked over to where he sat, but before she could take a look at the drawing, he reached out and pulled her to him. When he was sitting down, his face was on a level with hers. She was just about to say, "Well?" when his mouth closed over hers, and she was astounded by the intensity of his kiss. This wasn't nice-guy Harry anymore; this was seriously sensuous.

When he finally broke it off, he said, "So you see, I'm human, too. As for being a goody-goody..." He kissed her again and she began to forget all about negotiating. Surely there were better things to do than sit around arguing, particularly when she would rather be arguing his side than Kingsley's.

She leaned into him and wrapped her arms around his neck. She was alone with Harry in a barricaded building. If she played her cards right, the negotiations could last for days.

Unfortunately, the phone rang. Harry pulled away, saying, "You expecting a call?"

Jas shook her head.

Harry reached out for the phone with one hand while he kept the other firmly around her. That was okay with her; there was nowhere she'd rather be.

"No, I didn't," she heard Harry say. Then he gave her a look that could have been suspicious or could have been lustful, depending on how paranoid she felt like being.

She was just deciding on lustful when he hung up and said, "I can't trust you for a minute, can I?"

She didn't know what he was talking about. She hadn't moved away from him, had she?

"Don't give me that innocent look, Jas. That was the pizza place. They couldn't deliver because no one's allowed to enter the building."

"The pizza was for you, Harry. I just wanted a beer."

Harry took her firmly by the shoulders, turned her around and headed her back in the direction of the couch. "I can't be bought with pizza, Jas, and I can't be bought with kisses."

Jas sat down on the couch and glared at him. "Did I come over there and attack you, Harry? Did you or did you not lure me over there and then kiss me?"

"I was only proving a point."

"With the first kiss, maybe; not with the second. Anyway, all you did was kiss me. Big deal. If you were really trying to prove you're no saint, you would've done more than just kiss me."

Harry's eyes took on a gleam. "That sounds to me like a dare."

Jas shrugged.

"I haven't been dared by a female since the sixth grade, when Joanie Sarnowski dared me to chase her behind the bushes."

Jas felt a little uncomfortable with that. She had dared a few boys behind the bushes herself.

"You know what I'd do with most women, Jas? I'd simply take the woman's hand and lead her to the bedroom. Now with a few, of course, that wouldn't work. They would want the romantic gesture, something like picking them up and carrying them into the bedroom, thus protecting their image as the weaker sex."

Jas snorted.

"With you, however, I get the feeling it's going to be arm wrestling first."

Jas fought the urge to laugh and lost. "You really are a goody-goody. Why the bedroom? Is that the only room you ever have sex in?"

"You're really asking for it, aren't you?"

Jas shook her head.

"You're lying. You're still lying to me. I swear to God, you act like a twelve-year-old. You want to kiss the boy, but you won't admit it so instead you beat him up."

Jas thought that uncannily close to the mark.

Harry stood up and raised his fists. "Come on, you want to fight?"

"Just verbally, Harry, and I'd rather negotiate than fight."

Harry got down on the floor. "Want to decide the negotiations over who wins at arm wrestling?"

Jas had never lost at arm wrestling. On the other hand, she had stopped at the age when the boys got bigger than she was.

Still, a challenge was a challenge. She got down on the floor facing Harry, her right arm next to his. When he tried to clasp her hand, she grabbed his thumb and began to bend it back.

"I should've known you'd cheat," said Harry.

Jas slammed his arm to the floor. "I won," she said.

"You didn't win. You cheated."

"That's the way we always played," said Jas.

"Let me show you how we played," said Harry, grabbing her wrists and pinning them above her head, then straddling her.

"Oh, this kind of wrestling," said Jas, smiling up at him.

"If it makes you feel better to call it that, go ahead," said Harry.

"Okay, Harry, listen to me a minute, will you? Oh, Harry, come on, we'll have plenty of time to do that later."

Harry was unbuckling his belt. "We have plenty of time to do it now."

"Just let me say one thing, Harry. What if I could talk Kingsley into giving you your own co-op?"

"You know something, Jas? You kiss a hell of a lot better than you negotiate."

"Is that a no?"

"That's a no."

"Harry, what are you doing? Can't you at least leave your clothes on until we're through negotiating?"

"COULD WE RELAX for just a minute, Harry?"

"Are you kidding? I'm so relaxed I feel like I'm floating."

"You feel that way, too?"

"Sorry Grogan attacked you like that."

"Your attack more than made up for it."

"Want to move this show into the bedroom?"

"Harry, please, I'm supposed to be working. Why don't I give you his final offer?"

Harry rolled away from her. "Wait just a minute. You mean there was a final offer and I haven't heard it yet?"

"You don't start negotiations off with a final offer, Harry."

"Maybe not with an enemy you don't."

"Not with anyone."

"You're still not being honest with me, Jas. I don't believe it. We just made love, and you're still being devious."

Jas sat up and reached for her clothes. "You can't take this personally, Harry."

"What do you mean I can't take it personally? I'm in love with you, and you're still treating me like the enemy."

Jas paused with one arm in her sweat shirt. "You're in love with me?"

"No, I wrestle *all* women to the floor."

Jas pulled her arm out of the sweat shirt and bridged the gap between them. "Tell me again," she said.

"Tell you what?"

"What you just said. That you love me."

"I don't recall hearing a reciprocal declaration."

"Do you think I make love with people as part of my job? I'm not Mata Hari, for God's sake."

"Somehow I'm not totally convinced by your saying that."

"You never believe anything I say, anyway."

"That's not true. I've believed most of what you've said. It's just that it's all turned out to be lies."

"I don't want to tell you I love you. You'll just think it's another lie."

"I don't even believe that," said Harry. "I think the real reason you don't want to tell me is that you picture yourself as some hard-bitten private eye who's too macho to tell someone you love him."

"You're right," Jas admitted.

"But you'll make an exception in my case, won't you?"

"Okay," said Jas. "I love you." It had taken more courage than climbing out on the ledge, but once she had said it, she was so relieved she couldn't seem to stop. "I really do. I really love you, Harry. I love you; do you hear me?"

"I hear you. Now let's hear the final offer."

HARRY MOVED OFF HER and rolled over onto his back. "Yes, very nice—I'll take that offer anytime. But now I'd like to hear Kingsley's offer. The bottom line, okay?"

Jas was feeling almost too euphoric to get back to business. She couldn't remember when she had enjoyed her job so much. "Kingsley will let your building remain rental units if you'll call a truce."

"That's it?"

Jas got up on one elbow and looked down at his face. "It means you won. That's what you wanted, isn't it?"

"That's what it started off as, but now it's become a cause."

"You're being ridiculous, Harry. Legally, Kingsley could demolish you. But because he's a business man, and because you're losing him money, he's willing to make an exception on your building."

"I'd feel like I was copping out."

"You really weren't interested in negotiating when you invited me in here, were you?"

"Maybe initially, but I seem to have developed other interests. Like this," he said, pulling her over on top of him.

"Harry, look at it this way. You started it and you'll be able to show the other people it can be done. I'm sure they'll be able to carry on without you."

"They need Grogan."

"Enough's enough, Harry. Do you think people outside of New York are going to be interested in Grogan's building going co-op forever? It loses its humor after a few days."

"Do you really think so?"

"And there's no way all the real-estate developers are going to suddenly give the buildings back to the tenants."

"I know that, Jas."

"So can I call Kingsley and say we've reached an agreement?"

"I can't believe I'm in love with a detective."

"I'm called an investigator, Harry."

"You wouldn't consider doing something else for a living, would you?"

"No."

"That's what I figured."

"So is it a deal?"

"Come closer and I'll give you my answer."

"Just give me a yes or a no, keeping in mind that if it's a no, I'm going to have to leave and report in to Kingsley."

"Yes."

"You mean that?"

"I won. I really did. I beat Kingsley. Come over here and let's celebrate."

"Harry, stop that. Please, Harry, just let me make one telephone call first. Harry, will you get that cat away from me? Now he's biting my ankles."

Epilogue

The first frame showed Grogan, garbed in a silly-looking apron, cleaning up his co-op. Dust was sticking to his whiskers and his tail. The expression on Grogan's face was expectant.

The second frame showed Grogan hiding his apron as the Siamese cat appeared at his window with several pieces of luggage. Grogan was looking hot and bothered; the Siamese was looking cool.

The third frame showed Grogan reaching out his paws and carrying the Siamese cat over the window-sill and into his co-op. The Siamese looked coy; Grogan looked bewildered.

The last frame showed Grogan and the Siamese toasting each other with champagne. They both looked enchanted.

Harlequin Intrigue

In October
Watch for the new look of

Harlequin Intrigue

...because romance can be quite an adventure!

Each time, Harlequin Intrigue brings you great stories, mixing a contemporary, sophisticated romance with the surprising twists and turns of a puzzler...romance with "something more."

Plus...
in next month's publications of Harlequin Intrigue we offer you the chance to win one of four mysterious and exciting weekends. Don't miss the opportunity! Read the October Harlequin Intrigues!

Harlequin American Romance

COMING NEXT MONTH

#217 FOREVER FRIENDS By Patricia Cox

Cassie was convinced her plan would work! With her best friend Dave helping, what could go wrong? Plenty! Camping in the wilderness with bears and eating dried food wasn't what she had in mind! What started as a foolproof plan to get her man turned into the survival of the fittest.

#218 UNLIKELY PARTNERS by Jacqueline Diamond

Shy librarian Sarah Farentino was suddenly leading a Cinderella-like existence when she agreed to help handsome executive Michael McCord search for a missing heiress. But what would happen when the clock struck twelve?

#219 LOVE AND LAVENDER by Muriel Jensen

Arthur of Camelot? Will thought he'd heard wrong. He only wanted to rent a room from Rosie and make a fresh start—not fulfill her fantasy. Never in his wildest dreams did he envision meeting a woman who froze her credit cards and made strange concoctions with herbs!

#220 WHEN HEARTS DREAM by Laurel Pace

Major setbacks hadn't stopped Anne from opening a boutique, and pressure-filled days as an engineer didn't deter Wes from moonlighting as a jazz musician. With Anne's enthusiasm and Wes's unique energy, love should have been a dream come true. Instead, it was the most elusive dream of all.

Six exciting series for you every month... from Harlequin

Harlequin Romance.
The series that started it all

Tender, captivating and heartwarming...
love stories that sweep you off to faraway places
and delight you with the magic of love.

◆

Harlequin Presents.
Powerful contemporary love stories...as individual as the women who read them

The No. 1 romance series...
exciting love stories for you, the woman of today...
a rare blend of passion and dramatic realism.

◆

Harlequin Superromance®
It's more than romance... it's Harlequin Superromance

A sophisticated, contemporary romance-fiction
series, providing you with a longer,
more involving read...a richer mix of complex plots,
realism and adventure.

Harlequin
American Romance™
Harlequin celebrates the American woman…

…by offering you romance stories written about American women, by American women for American women. This series offers you contemporary romances uniquely North American in flavor and appeal.

◆

Harlequin Temptation™
Passionate stories for today's woman

An exciting series of sensual, mature stories of love…dilemmas, choices, resolutions… all contemporary issues dealt with in a true-to-life fashion by some of your favorite authors.

◆

Harlequin Intrigue
Because romance can be quite an adventure

Harlequin Intrigue, an innovative series that blends the romance you expect… with the unexpected. Each story has an added element of intrigue that provides a new twist to the Harlequin tradition of romance excellence.

Harlequin Books®

PROD-A-2

Can you keep a secret?

You can keep this one plus 4 free novels